AF528352

Faraway Yet Closer

Faraway Yet Closer
Written by Amina Hazim
Print Edition

First Published in India in 2021
Inkfeathers Publishing
New Delhi 110095

Copyright © Amina Hazim, 2021
Cover Design © Amina Hazim, 2021
Cover Image © Pexels.com

All rights reserved.

ISBN 978-93-90882-03-8

Without limiting the rights under copyright reserved above, no part of this publication may be reproduced, lent, resold, or transmitted by any means, electronic, mechanical, photocopying or otherwise, without the prior permission of both the copyright owner and the publisher of this book.

www.inkfeathers.com

Faraway Yet Closer

AMINA HAZIM

Inkfeathers Publishing

CONTENTS

Chapter 1 1
Chapter 2 14
Chapter 3 30
Chapter 4 39
Chapter 5 43
Chapter 6 49
Chapter 7 55
Chapter 8 60
Chapter 9 64
Chapter 10 68
Chapter 11 75
Chapter 12 85
Chapter 13 89
Chapter 14 95
Chapter 15 101
Chapter 16 111
Chapter 17 120
Chapter 18 124
Chapter 19 128

Chapter 20 132
Chapter 21 144
Chapter 22 152
Chapter 23 159
Chapter 24 166
Chapter 25 174
Chapter 26 181
Chapter 27 187
Chapter 28 193

Meet the Author 197
Acknowledgements 198

1

"Alina! Dinner is ready."

I heard my mom calling me from downstairs.

"Coming, mom." I replied.

Now where did I keep my nail polish? Oh, there it is! I think I will do my nails after dinner.

As I got down the stairs, there stood a slim figure, dressed immaculately, who even at the age of 40, would never compromise with her taste in fashion.

Oh right! It's none other than my beloved mother.

"Mom, where is dad? Isn't he coming home for dinner tonight?" I asked her as I eased myself onto a chair. "No honey, he has a business meeting in London. His flight leaves in an hour," she replied as she took a sip of her wine.

"Oh right, I forgot that."

I finished my dinner, accompanied only by the silence of my mom and the clattering of the cutleries. After helping her with the dishes, I planted a kiss on her cheeks and headed upstairs. "Goodnight, mom! I am going to bed," I announced as I ran up.

"Alina, it's Saturday. Don't you have any plans?"

"Later, maybe."

Back in my room, I closed the door behind me and took a deep breath. A pile of books waited for me on the desk. *Oh God I hate my life! Why are there so many assignments on my plate again?*

Oh, right! I keep procrastinating. Well, complaining won't do the trick, huh?

I dragged myself to my desk and started working. I was halfway done with my assignments when the phone rang. The ringtone tore through the silence and startled me, almost making me jump. It was Jessica.

Now what could she want from me?

"Hey Al! Where are you at?" Her voice chimed through the receiver.

"Hanging by a cliff on Everest. Care to join?"

"Your attempt at sarcasm is pitiful. Now. What are you doing at home on a Saturday night? Did God really have to put all dimwits in my friend circle?"

"Some people have homework, Jessica. What is it that you want on a 'Saturday Night'?"

"Well, for one, Jake is having a party at his place tonight, so I want you to join. And second, I don't want people working on a Saturday night!"

"Yeah right. Whatever. Pick me up in 30 minutes. I will get back by 11 and deal with my stuff."

"That's like my Al!" She squealed with joy.

Sometimes she really is proud of me. Or was that bad sarcasm again?

A quick shower and I was ready for the night. The good thing about late night parties was that makeup didn't matter. Among all those neon lights, anyone hardly noticed. So I looked pretty enough in my knee length red dress and minimal makeup.

I walked down the stairs cautiously in my black heels just to find my mom and Jessica giggling about something.

"There you are!" Jessica exclaimed.

"And there we go," I started walking out.

"Bye, Linda!" Jessica blew a kiss to my mom.

"Be back soon Alina," I heard her call out.

"I'll be back by eleven."

Geez. When did I become so responsible?

We drove a few blocks and took a turn. The long queue of cars waiting to enter the lane, and the music that could be heard even from two blocks away has set the ambience well enough.

"The queue is too long, Jess. I don't have enough time," I whined. "Why don't you just call Jake and tell him we are here?"

"Yeah, I can do that." She took out her phone and dialled a few digits. I tapped my toe to the beats as she waited for Jack to pick up.

We were in before we knew it. You see, when you have an option of being special and elite, never lose it.

The music blared in my ears as we entered the driveway. I scanned the area just to see random teens making out in every possible corner.

I would never host a party where random mates can just crash in. I mean, gold laced invitation cards are a must, eh? And what kind of cocktail smells like that? Geez!

With all those thoughts running back and forth in my mind, I hardly paid attention to the people around who were making way for us as we walked in. When someone is rich and popular since her childhood, it doesn't become a habit to ignore the special treatment, rather it becomes 'normal'. It was nothing new for me, neither the silver spoon I was born with, nor the exotic life I led thereafter. It's the same on both sides, either you get used to being poor, or you get used to being rich. It's normal either way.

I love hanging out by the kitchen when it comes to parties. Especially at Jack's house. As we entered it and the smell of baked bread and herbs filled my head, I noticed a boy standing by the refrigerator, having his drink.

Is it really the kitchen or is it him smelling so delicious?

He was around six feet tall, and his perfect physique along with his broad shoulders was accompanied well by sandy brown hair.

Am I really complimenting him as a dish now?

"Jake!" Jessica had to ruin the moment. She spotted Jake and jumped right into his arms, and before I turned towards them, they had already started to make out.

Jess always has to ruin it. No, like really, ruin it.

"Guys come on! At Least have some privacy. There's someone else in this room," I said, and Jessica just giggled.

Did she giggle at my protest or is it just Jake's lips running on her neck? Either ways - Ugh!

Jake pulled himself away from her just to throw his arms around me.

Bear hug incoming!

"Al! Thanks for coming!" He said as he squeezed the life out of me.

"Where are Sam and Victoria? Shouldn't they be here by now?"

"They couldn't make it."

"Because...?"

"They are at Vic's, having dinner with her parents."

"Oh, Okay! You guys carry on. I will go get a drink. But Jess, we are leaving by 11, alright?"

"Tick-tock, Al! Got it!" She sounded too excited.

I came outside and started walking by the pool as it was the most quiet place I could find. The music was suppressed by the thick glass walls and the fresh air helped me escape the smell of cheap cocktails back inside.

As I scrolled through my Instagram and tried walking straight, I bumped into something. Well that something turned out to be 'someone'. My eyes landed on the forest green eyes of the last person I would've liked to see, Keely Lawrence. I was irked from my core, and she could sense it well enough because I made it obvious through my facial expression.

"Watch where you're going!"

"Really? Or maybe next time you can stick those eyes on the road rather than in that cell phone of yours. And also, just because your father owns a few shares doesn't mean you own the country."

She shouldn't have done that.

"Well you see, Keely, I don't own America, but I also don't go around and tell people about the 50% my father owns. You know why? 'cause you do that job for me!"

She feels destroyed. I can see it on her face.

"You won't last long in the business, Campbell." She scorned at me and started walking away, her eyes pinned at her cell phone.

"Well, we will see about that. Lawrence! Won't we?"

No reply? Who's walking with her eyes on the phone now?

I walked back into the house. That small catfight had left me with no other choice but to reunite with my friends and find something to drink. Jake and Jess were sitting on the kitchen island. I could hear them murmuring something about the upcoming summer ball. I went straight for the refrigerator and took out a carton of juice. "Hmmph! I could really use a drink right now," I announced and started gulping the sweet orange juice.

"Hey Al, who are you going with to the ball this year?" Jake asked.

"Options are not limited, Jake, but I think I will decide later," I concluded as I took a seat nearby. "Maybe you should go with Noah. Or are you planning to go solo?" Jess asked me with an 'I know it already' smile.

"Maybe. Maybe not. But you know what? We should leave now." I checked my watch just to remind myself of the assignments waiting for me at my desk.

"Okay! Bye, Jake!"

After exchanging one or two silly jokes and bidding goodbyes, we finally left. Jessica dropped me by my house and drove away. I kept looking at the car going away until I could see nothing but hear the rumble.

With a sigh, I looked at my driveway just to see a BMW parked outside. The latest model with modifications for comfort?

Dad?

"Dad!" I ran inside and hugged him. He sat there, reading one of his dusty, old, leathered books. No matter if he owns Campbell Ltd., he has always been down to earth and loved the scent of his old books. "Never be proud of what you own, Al. Always be happy about what you can give," he would say this to me every now and then just to remind me of not taking anything for granted.

"Alina, I was gone only for a few days and you miss me already?!" He laughed.

"Well the days felt like years, so yes! Of Course I missed you so much!"

He giggled at me as I made a puppy face.

Oh I love him!

"I love you, Dad!"

"I love you too, Sweetheart!" He smiled as if in peace. "Oh! And I think I have a perfect birthday gift for you." He fumbled for something in his coat, took out an envelope and handed it over to me. I sat on my knees, confused and excited, as I tore it open.

Three plane tickets to France? Wait, three business class tickets to France?!

"Do you like it?" He asked hopefully.

"Like it? I love it dad! Thank You so much!" I jumped and hugged him again.

"We leave two days prior to your birthday, alright? So that leaves you with two weeks to pack up!" The best part about my birthday is that the summer vacations always fall around it, thus making me feel like flying!

The next day started as usual. The alarm went off at 6;45, and before I was fully awake, I found myself in the kitchen. Dad was sitting at the table with his newspaper, and mom was busy with her nail. I exchanged kisses and grabbed the car keys.

It's fun racing the bus till school.

Waywood academy is the most prestigious school in Greenville. And the expensiveness is nothing but a compliment. Whether it be the imported floor tiles from Italy, or the crystal chandeliers illuminating the hallway, everything in Waywood whispered 'money'. There are no lock systems for the lockers. Instead, you just scan your thumb for access.

Technology is the science of privilege, eh?

The classrooms are well maintained and situated in the main building of the 600 acres campus. The east and the west wing are used for a fancy cafeteria and a library along with state-of-the-art laboratories respectively.

How perfect can a school be, huh? And why not? We pay such a huge amount every year for the best education possible. And all we learn is socializing.

I took a few books from my locker and headed towards the class for the first period. "Hey Al wait up!" Jessica called me from behind, her hair bobbing as she jogged towards me.

"Morning, Jess!"

"So, where are you going this year?"

"Well last night my dad surprised me with tickets to France."

She squealed in excitement. She seemed more enthused than I was.

"And guess what? When I come back, I am gonna take you guys to London. My treat!"

Her squeal of joy resumed but was suppressed by the corridor bell. It really seemed as if her squeal rang like a bell.

"Will see you at lunch Al!" She jogged away.

At lunch time, the cafe usually gets too crowded, but the central table would always remain unoccupied as if it waited for us. I could see my friend group seated around the table as I made my way towards them with my plate of buns and jam.

The day couldn't have been more exhausting. Four lectures with an empty stomach? No doubt my pen's cap is chewed off!

"Guys, listen up! For my birthday I am planning something huge. A trip to London! Who's in?"

"Yeah!" They all cheered together. Victoria nodded as Sam kept chanting, "I'm in!"

"It's gonna be nothing but fun."

"Couldn't agree more Al!" Jack raised his tetra pak, "To Al!"

"To Al!" Others joined in.

To long lives and London!

Only four days left for France, and I am still left with so much to pack!

I walked down the stairs and into the living room, wondering what else I could have missed to pack. Mom was sitting on her armchair with a book in her hand.

And that is not a good sign. Mom reading books means she is not in a good mood. And mom reading with her legs crossed means 'Dad argued'.

"Alina, can I talk to you?"

Knew it.

"What is it, Mom?"

"Look, I know it's your birthday and you are really excited for this trip, and I want you to enjoy it to your fullest. But honey, I am really sorry, I won't be able to come."

"Just because you had a stupid fight again?"

She glared at me, "Alina. Don't you talk back like that! Ask one of your friends to join in."

"But Mom…"

"No more arguments. I am done with it."

She never understands. Does she?

"Fine! I will ask Jess to come with me! And I will make sure I don't miss you!"

"Good for you." She said as she walked away.

Not a good time for sarcasm Mom! I know I sound stupid when I am pissed.

I stormed out of the living room and stomped intentionally on each stair I climbed to make her realize how angry I really was. Everytime they have a little fight, I am the one who pays for it. And the bitter truth is they always mend things up even before I realize it, and I am left wondering why was I dragged in anyways?

The good part of me being pissed is that I finish up my pending work a lot faster than I would have done before in normal conditions. And thus, I was finished with my packing by afternoon.

Maybe it's high time that I call Jessica and tell her to pack up. Mom is not changing her mind sooner.

The appreciable thing about Jessica is that I can count on her. And the best part about her is that I can *forever* count on her.

"Of course, I will come with you Al!" I heard her squeal through the receiver.

God how perfect can friendship be, eh?

Friday came up soon and we were on our way to the airport. Dad sat beside me, a big smile on his face as if it were his birthday surprise. I didn't feel like asking anything that could ruin his mood, but then again, I was helpless. "Dad, what happened between you and mom?"

Yeah. I saw that. The smile dropped off his face like a glass from someone's hand.

"Oh, it's nothing dear. Just some usual argument."

Well if you don't wanna say, I don't wanna poke.

The car stopped at the entrance. I saw Jessica standing by the drop off point.

"Hi, Al!" She came running and hugged me until I suffocated. "This is gonna be so much fun Al! You, me and Paris!!"

"Well, hello there Jessica." The smile on my Dad's face returned.

"Mr. Campbell, thank you so much for letting me come." To which my Dad's smile broadened.

Paris looked like a land embedded with pearls up from the night sky. I have been to so many countries, but this was the first time in France. The beauty of Paris lies almost on anything your eyes fall on. Whether it be the romantic lights, the historical buildings, or the unique sense of fashion, everything can make one feel mesmerized.

Peninsula Paris, the hotel where we stayed was one of the hotels that provided five-star services.

If you want assured comfort served with etiquettes of hospitality, what better place you could choose?!

The day that followed our arrival was spent mostly on shopping and sight-seeing, and by the time we returned to our rooms, we were too exhausted. Jessica made her way straight to bed, while I decided to go and check on my dad. He was standing outside, next to the elevator. "Dad?" I walked towards him and he ushered me into the elevator. "Dad, I'm exhausted. Can't we do this tomorrow?"

"Yes, if you want to miss it."

And then he covered my eyes. We walked out of the elevator and I felt a cold breeze around my cheeks. "Dad, are we on the terrace?"

"Hush. Keep walking honey."

And then he finally moved his hands away, revealing the surprise. There were fairy lights wrapped around the rooftop pillars, and a floral arch stood right in the middle of all the lights. And then there was the decorated table behind it, with my giant birthday cake sitting on it - ready to be cherished.

Oh my God! What could be more surprising than this...

"Happy birthday, Al!" Jessica jumped out from behind the table.

I was so wrong!

"So what happened to all that 'I am exhausted to death' drama eh?" I laughed as she came and gave me her 'choke hug'.

How excited can she become huh?!

"Come on, Al! Go ahead and cut the cake," Dad nudged me forward. As I cut the cake and blew the candles, I noticed tears in his eyes. "My munchkin has grown up eh!"

He wiped away his tears and bit on the piece of cake I offered him. Then he put some icing on my nose, and I simply giggled. "Now it's time for a present."

"What is it Dad?"

He took out a classy, leather coated, small box out of his pocket and handed it over to me. "Why don't you open it and tell me?"

I flipped the box open and took out a beautiful chain. It was a thin gold chain with a heart shaped pendant and embedded diamonds over it. The pendant swung open and a family picture came into view that dad had taken last year.

"So?" He took it from my hand and put it around my neck. "Do you like it?"

"Dad, this is so beautiful! I am going to keep this with me forever! I love you so much!" And I hugged him.

"I love you too, Munchkin!"

This will be my best birthday. No matter how much celebration I have in future, this, right here, will remain the best.

After an unforgettable night and a quick trip the next day, we came back to America. Mom and Jake were waiting for us at the airport. Mom waved at me frantically with one hand, and in the other hand I saw, she held a wrapped present.

"Happy belated birthday, Sweetheart!" She blew a kiss to me and handed over the present. "I am really sorry I couldn't make it there baby."

"Yeah. Whatever," I gave her a sarcastic smile and turned to Jake. "Did you miss me?!"

Shouldn't have asked that. Bear hug incoming!

I exchanged goodbye kisses with them and left with my parents. The following week dad left for a business trip. "I will be back soon Alina. And then book the tickets for London. Until then be a good girl." He then kissed Mom goodbye. "If you need anything, call me, alright?" She nodded. Their argument had sorted but one could feel the coldness between them. And then as I stood by the driveway, he smiled at me and left.

I wonder what brings out his smile that I can die for.

2

"So. Which shop do we hit first?" Jessica asked from the back seat. We had been driving for a long time monotonously before Victoria announced the day as a 'shopping day'. The boys were having their soccer practice under the sun, unlike us, who preferred to sit in my luxurious Audi and complain about hardships in life.

Doing nothing is hard enough, eh?

"Well we can visit Prada. I hear they are launching their summer collections today," Victoria turned to me for affirmation. "Well that sounds worth a long drive," I agreed and steered into a different lane.

Prada took longer to reach than I expected, but then again it was worth it. The girls moved onto the handbag section, having a mild debate on what would suit over a lime yellow top while I was more attracted to shoes. I feel butterflies in my belly whenever I find a new collection of it.

You see, they define my personality somehow.

I heard my phone ring after we checked out. It's a difficult job to pick up the phone while carrying all those bought burdens in carry bags. "Jolie?" I wondered out loud.

Why would she call me? She never calls me until it's something about Dad.

"Ms. Campbell, I am really sorry to inform you that…" She couldn't complete her sentence. I heard her weeping over the receiver. "

"Jolie, what is it?" I could feel by heart throbbing in my chest as if it knew before me that something bad had happened. "Ms. Campbell, it's your father. He met with an accident. Please come over as soon as possible." Her voice started to fade away as if someone had punctured my senses. My ears turned red hot and I could feel my legs tremble, and before I could utter another word, I fell down as if I were floating. I could hear Jessica screaming my name, and then I heard Victoria talking to Jolie over my phone. "Jess, we have to take her home first. Linda is not picking up her call. She has no idea about this."

Somehow I regained my senses and Jessica drove us to my house. My mom was busy cooking and had not bothered to answer Jolie's calls. Everything after that was nothing but a blur, until I finally found myself sitting outside the Intensive Care Unit, waiting for the nurse to call us in.

"It will be alright, Al. Your dad will be fine," Victoria tried to console me but I felt miserable and just wanted to curl into a ball and just lie there, forever. I didn't want to see my dad stitched up and covered in bandages. I didn't want to see him struggling to breathe through that oxygen mask, or fighting every second for a second chance. But then the nurse called us in, and I pushed myself forward just to see my father wrapped in bandages and covered with life supporting machineries. My mom passed by me as I entered the unit, as only one visitor was allowed at a time. She looked so pale, as if she had seen the worst of her life, and I was about to witness the worst of mine.

Dad lied on his bed, surprisingly peaceful. He looked so frail and small, and his face was hardly visible with all those bandages wrapped up around his head.

"The doctors are trying everything they can, Mrs. Campbell." I could hear the nurse explaining the situation to my mom. "But the patient has multiple internal injuries." Slowly I walked over to my dad and stopped halfway, not knowing what to do. Then he opened his eyes and looked at me. That man was standing at the doorstep of death, and he looked so peaceful, while I stood there, alive and fit, but trembling inside out.

"Hey, Munchkin," he said in a voice that was as dry as cotton.

I sat beside him, my eyes filled with tears, and my body ready to sink beneath the harsh reality. "Dad, what happened?"

"Oh, it's nothing Alina. Just had a bad day."

"Dad don't worry, we will do everything to fix this." Tears ran down my cheeks as I held his hand. It felt cold. Very cold. His lips curled to deliver a faint effortless smile, and I could hear him wheezing. "Baby, you promise me one thing, okay?"

"Anything Dad."

"You will be strong after I am gone."

"Dad, no! You are not going anywhere. We will take you to the best doctors and also give you the best treatment."

"I think I have done that already. This is inevitable dear. The pain is unbearable, but you know the funny part? I don't feel it anymore." And he winked as if he were mocking death. "You be brave Alina. You take care of your mother. We have had our arguments but she's the memory of love I am taking with myself."

I couldn't take it anymore. His voice started ringing in my ears. I couldn't believe how easily he had accepted death. A renowned man, with a wealth that could feed half the planet, was lying there helpless in front of his family, letting death take away everything he has ever earned.

"Now listen to me. I have talked to Lawrence and he has promised me he will take care of you and your mother. All my wealth is now under your possession. I have taken care of everything dear. I mean it, everything! You won't lose anything at all."

"And what about you Dad? Am I not losing you?"

"No, dear. I will be there with you. Always. I will even bring you salty potato chips," he started to giggle and ended up coughing. I looked at his eyes as it started to lose its shine. His grip started to loosen and I felt so helpless. I wanted to hold onto him, and not let him go away, ever. But some things are like the flying cotton tufts from the kapok trees, the more you try to catch it, the more it gets away. His wheezing fainted slowly, and then his glance turned into a cold stare. There was silence for a moment and then it was taken over by the cardiac event monitor's constant beep tone. I sat there, frozen to the floor, as if I had been there forever.

Outside the room, stood a woman whose husband has left her with everything but happiness, a team of highly skilled doctors who might have saved a million lives but couldn't help just another man because destiny had other plans, and a couple of friends who doubted that their friend would smile ever again.

Money can literally buy everything but can't hold onto anything.

The next few days seemed like a long bad dream. Every now and then, I would wonder what would happen if Dad came over to my bed and planted a kiss to wake me up from this bad dream. Oh I would have hugged him so hard, and never let go off him ever again. Maybe I should have been a bit stubborn and stopped him back at the airport. He would have stopped. He loved me. I could have saved him.

Come on, Dad! Just plant a kiss on my forehead and wake me up. I wanna wake up Dad, just to sleep again on your lap and dream better this time.

But time passed, even though I was not ready to accept it. We flew to London for the funeral. It was filled with unfamiliar faces more than familiar ones. Dad's connections were much broader than I would have ever guessed. Faces that we never acquainted came up and gave us condolences. And then there were my friends who stood beside me the entire time. I leaned over Jessica as I walked to my dad's coffin which was lying still in its grave.

"Ashes to ashes, dust to dust," the priest said out loud as I poured a handful of soil over the coffin. And that was the only memory of the funeral that stayed in my heart.

Back at my house, Mom locked herself up as soon as we entered. She had her own ways of dealing with grief. And for a teenager like me, I would say that grief was just introduced to my life and thus, I had no ways of dealing with it. So, I lied on my bed and let all my tears out, hoping it would take away the pain. I cried for hours, before I finally got exhausted and fell into a dreamless sleep.

I woke up with a horrible headache and a sore throat. For a moment I forgot everything that had happened earlier, but then it all came back at once. It felt as if someone was pelting my heart with all the bad memories. My guts wrenched as the thought of never seeing dad again occurred in my mind, and my limbs went numb. It wasn't a dream after all.

Aren't you going to walk through that door?

I took a shower and went downstairs to find mom. She was not in the living room.

Must be still sleeping.

I wanted her to be with me, but she likes to be left alone when in grief. I was not interested to reply to the numerous unread messages on my phone, so I walked out into the garden to get some fresh air. The fragrance of sweet peas welcomed me into the garden and the fresh air heaved my sunken heart. And as I walked on the soft grass, a Black Mercedes came into my driveway and stopped. A tall man with peppered hair, wearing a dark black suit stepped out of the car and walked towards me. Two more men stepped out of the car and followed him in silence.

"Hello Alina, nice meeting you, I'm James Pallmer, your father's lawyer. Is your mother at home?" he said.

"Yes, come on in," I led them back into the house and into the living room. Once they were all seated, I said, "Can you wait a few minutes, I'll let mom know you're here." I headed upstairs to my mother's bedroom. When I got to her room, I knocked a few times softly on the door, but when there was no response, I opened it anyway. I slowly made my way to the night lamp and switched it on as the room was pitch dark.

"Oh my god, turn off that light, can't you see someone is sleeping here?" She grumbled at me from her bed. "Mom, get up. It's one in the afternoon and Dad's solicitor is already here."

She got up from the bed and slowly made her way to the bathroom. "Make them some coffee. I will be downstairs in 10 minutes," She mumbled and went away.

I came back with a pot of coffee a few minutes later and as I entered, Mom walked down into the living room as well. The lawyer got up from his seat to shake hands with her, "Mrs. Campbell, nice to meet you. My name is James Pallmer and I am here to discuss with you about Mr. Campbell's will that he has left behind."

"Yes, please have a seat." Mom eased herself on the couch. "Tell me Mr. Pallmer. What is it?"

"Well ma'am, it looks like your husband has signed all his properties to a person named Daimen Lawrence that he had mentioned is his friend. I am sorry to say this but it's a signed will and it clearly implies that he hasn't left any of his properties in America for his daughter and you."

I was shocked to the very core of my heart. It took me more than a while to realize what has happened. I had never faced anything like this before.

Dad would never do this. Would he?

I looked at mom. Her Face had turned pale and it seemed as if she had been standing frozen to the ground for decades.

"Dad told me… before passing away… that…"

"Ms. Alina, we were informed of the same and thought that everything is left under your name. But today morning, Mr. Damien Lawrence came to our office with the will papers duly signed by Mr. Campbell and it clearly states that now, after the unfortunate demise of him, all his properties shall be named under Lawrence and that now the true owner of Campbell Ltd. is none other than Lawrence himself." "But the papers might be forged! Why don't you investigate that?" My voice trembled with fear and uncertainty. I looked at mom helplessly, just to see her stand up calmly. Her face was no more pale.

"Mom…"

"Well thank you, Mr. Pallmer, for explaining us the situation in hand. If that's all you came for, then I think we are done here," she extended her hand firmly and the lawyer stood up and shook it. With a smile, and a slight nod, Pallmer left the house with nothing but questions.

"Mom, why didn't you do something? Didn't you hear him? We are left with nothing!" I cried as she came over to me and held my hands. "Alina, darling." She replied. "I knew this day would come. I had warned your father long ago about Lawrence and his bad intentions, but he never paid attention. I always felt he was cooking something up, and today that day has come."

My throat went numb as I slowly realized we lost everything that my father had earned and built. "But Mom, the properties in London. How come they are still under our possession?"

She caressed my head with her hands and let out a deep sigh. "They are not under your dad's name, Alina. The properties in London are mine. We won't be going back to America anymore. From now on, we will stay here."

"But Mom!" I started to protest just to be interrupted by her rigidity. "I will start working as a paediatrician again, and you will have to find a new school."

"Mom, we can't just…"

"Your summer holidays end next week, Alina. I will take you to your new school after that."

"No one will take me in now. It's almost mid-term."

"I will contact Mattwood Academy. It's from where I passed out, and now you will too. Your father has left us with some money. We will go buy a ride for you tomorrow and then we are all set." And with that she left the room.

The next day, I got a brand-new car as promised. It was the latest model of BMW. Mom said we couldn't afford a sports car anymore, but she would let me choose the colour. And I chose black.

"What about you mom? Are you not buying one?"

"I will. Later. And by the way all our belongings are being shipped by Jolie. It will reach us by Friday."

"Maybe we should ask her about what happened. She was dad's secretary. She has to know something, huh?"

"Damien has sacked all of your father's loyal employees Alina. That company is long gone. So stop thinking about it." With that said, she finished signing all the documents for the car and walked away.

The next day.

"Mom! We are getting late." I stood on our driveway, waiting for her to come out. It was my first day at Mattwood and I didn't want to be late.

Ten minutes and yet no sign of her. Perfect mom, just perfect. How worse is the day going to be anyways?

She came out with a very hefty bag in her hand just when I was about to return inside to grab my car keys. "Come on sweetheart, now we don't want to be late on your first day right," she said as she climbed into the driver's seat whilst I climbed into the passenger seat.

"So tell me Al. Are you excited?" She tried to lighten up my mood as our car passed a few blocks of our new neighbourhood.

"Mattwood. Late already. No idea what's next. Yeah mom, I am too excited for this," I replied sarcastically.

We drove in silence for the next ten minutes or so. And then she tried to crack a conversation again. "So Alina, how about I come and pick you up after school?"

"Yeah cool."

And she failed miserably again. We entered the school's parking lot. It was huge with all kinds of unique cars parked around.

It's not going to be that bad eh?

The school building was crowded with students heading for their next class. My mom knocked on the Principal's door gently and entered.

"Oh Linda!" The Principal got up from her chair and hugged my mom. She gestured to us to sit down, and then she sat herself. "My dear, after such a long time! It's such a pleasure to see you."

"Same here, Laurel."

"Linda, I heard what happened to your husband. My deepest condolences goes to you and your daughter." She looked at me with pity. "Oh such a lovely and young child. Don't worry dear, God has its own ways." I gave a faint smile. "Here," she handed me a laminated sheet. "It's your class schedule. And if you need anything, let me know ok?" I nodded and turned to mom. "You guys know each other mom?"

"Yes. Laurel was my friend back in school days dear."

"And she was mine. A special one." Laurel smiled.

"Well that's good to know. I think i should be heading up for my first class now."

"Yes dear. All the very best to you." My mom planted a kiss on my cheek and I left the old friends alone just to begin my new journey.

I entered my first class. It was Biology. I walked to the very last bench with my head bent down to avoid any attention and then eased myself on an empty desk.

Just read your books and everything will be fine. No one sees you.

And then a girl sat beside me. I looked up to see a slim figure with honey blond hairs holding a smile on her face. "Hi, I am Poppy."

"Er... Hi, I am Alina."

Damn I tried so hard to avoid acquaintances.

And then Poppy turned out to be too friendly. It felt as if she was blabbering almost everything that came in her mind. The teacher finally relieved me from her blabbering with a sharp shush.

The bell rang and I grabbed my opportunity to escape Poppy's overfriendliness. "Hey Alina!" She called out as I walked through the corridor.

"What do you want?!"

Well that came out wrong eh?

"I just wanted to ask if we can have lunch together," she sounded lower than before. I realized she had felt my rudeness. "Look Poppy, thanks but I prefer to be left alone." I tried to sound as gentle as possible and then strode away towards my next class. "Okay, but the offer is still up!" I heard her shout from behind.

By the time lunch came I had lost half my energy. So I slowly moved to the cafeteria and desperately looked for a place to sit. The place was well maintained and had superior standards but was not as posh as my previous school's cafeteria.

I scanned the area once or twice until I finally spotted Poppy waving at me frantically. There were two more students sitting on that table, and in a moment they started waving at me as well. Not wanting to act weird and walk away, I was left with no other option but to walk to her with a forced smile on my face.

"Told you Alina, the offer was still up!"

I grinned at her and sat opposite to her. "Hi, everyone." I waved awkwardly at Poppy's friends. They all stared at me as if I were a fossil excavated from Mars.

This is exactly the weirdness that I was trying to avoid.

"So Alina, meet my friends," Poppy got up and started to introduce them one by one. "So this is Adrian and that's Lucy. And guys, this is Alina." Lucy was small and had black hair with a glowing olive skin while Adrian was tall and had brown curly hairs.

"So, where are you from Alina?" Adrian smiled at me.

"America."

"Oh cool. Did the A-listers approach you anyways?"

"Who?"

"The A-listers. They approach newcomers and bully them. You will know soon," he laughed.

"We are so happy you joined us Alina." Poppy chimed in trying to break the conversation about the A-listers. "Would you like to hang out with us at Starbucks after school? We go there usually," Lucy asked. "Yeah because someone likes watching Chris Franco for two hours straight," Adrian scoffed and Lucy gave her a short glare. Then she turned back to me with the same energy and smile, "What do you say Alina?"

i don't think so.

"Yeah sure. Thanks for inviting me!"

"That's great!" She patted me hard on my back. Lucy was stronger than she seemed to be.

I had chemistry the next period, so I went to the lab. Miss Clank, the lab teacher, matched me up with Adrian. And throughout, he was either making fun of me or cracking jokes, which, to be frank, made me laugh.

I promised myself I would not make any friends, but here I am.

And I must admit that Adrian is entertaining. "And Ally Tally is the best nickname for you." He announced and I tried to argue with him but eventually gave up.

After school, the four of us made our way to Adrian's Mercedes in the parking lot. While the three of them piled into Adrian's car, I said my goodbyes, had a brief conversation about the meet at Starbucks, and made my way to my mother's car. "How was school?" She inquired. "It was fine," I replied. "Did Alina make any new friends?" She wondered aloud. "Yes, and they invited me to join them at Starbucks later," I replied.

"That sounds great honey!" She exclaimed and I delivered back a smile.

I was almost 10 minutes late when I arrived at Starbucks. So when I parked my car and walked inside, I saw Adrian, Poppy, and Lucy drinking coffee in the far corner.

I bought myself a mocha and walked over to the table where they were seated. I took my seat next to Lucy.

"Hi Ally! We thought you wouldn't show up."

"And why is that?"

"Well Poppy was telling us how she was taken aback when you sounded rude to her," Adrian giggled. Poppy looked at me awkwardly. She felt embarrassed. "And why would you guys tell her that?" She rolled her eyes dramatically.

"Hey Poppy, I am sorry about that. I was not in a good mood today morning." I apologized, trying to save myself and her from awkwardness. "That's alright Ally. No offence taken. I was just worried about you."

And with that we hit random conversations and our evening started. I noticed Adrian had his hand wrapped around Poppy's shoulder and that made me curious. "So, you and Poppy have a thing eh?" I heard myself say that out loud.

Why Alina? Why would you think that out loud?

Adrian laughed and Poppy went beet red. "That took you long enough to figure out, Ally Tally," and he laughed some more. Lucy grinned at Poppy's blushing face and then turned to me, " They are dating from the last five years, but every time Poppy hears someone say or ask about it, she turns red as if it's something very new and she is not yet ready to reveal it.

"Oh that's so sweet Poppy," I smiled at her and she even turned more red. We talked a while about the usual rainy weather in London, and then out of the blues Adrian asked me, "So Alina, do you have a boyfriend?" Now it was my turn to face the attention. Three pairs of eyes stared at me, eagerly waiting for an answer. "Well... Ahem. No." Silence followed my answer for a while.

Are they expecting to hear something more?

"Oh, that's not a problem at all. We will find you one. There are a lot of boys roaming single in Mattwood anyways." Lucy said breaking the silence.

"Well thanks Lucy, but I think I am fine alone. I have a lot more things to do and am not really ready for a relationship.

Because last time I was dumped for not paying much attention to the relationship. Well, to be more specific I never loved him back.

"Hey Ally, do you want to carpool with us?" Adrian asked me. "Huh? Yeah that sounds good to me." I said, wondering if he was thinking that I don't have a car of my own. "Well it's not like you don't have a car and that's why I asked you to adjust with us," he said.

Did I speak my thoughts out loud?

"No but I do have a car of my own," I clarified. "You do? Well, that's great. We just do this for fun." Poppy replied. "On Mondays, it's Adrian's turn to drive, then I take the ball on

Tuesdays, and pass it onto Lucy on Wednesdays and that's how it keeps going."

"Well cool, count me in."

"Great. Then I will pick you up tomorrow," Poppy concluded.

"But you guys don't know where I live."

"Oh we know where you live," Lucy replied. "You live four houses ahead from Liam's."

"And who's Liam?"

"He is one of the A-listers," Adrian answered. "Well then I don't have anything to do with that I believe." I rolled my eyes showing my loss of curiosity.

"You think so Ally? Liam's one of them. Just imagine if you can join their group. You will rock," Lucy jumped up.

Well I have been one of the elites once. And it makes you nothing but a snobbish person and makes you judge everyone. If only I had understood it before, I would have more friends now than I already do.

"Well Ally Tally is thinking deep." Adrian said breaking my chain of thoughts. "What's this Ally Tally?" Poppy asked. "It's a stupid nickname your boyfriend gave me." I scoffed. "Hey come on, it's not stupid. It's cute." Adrian said and then whispered out loud, "Cute is stupid." And they laughed.

Surprisingly, so did I.

It made me wonder how alive and happy these people were after all. Back in America, my friends would never talk about anything but school and parties. It felt good to be a joke for the first time.

When I was going to leave I felt like I wanted another cup of mocha, so I went back inside to get one. And then as I turned to leave, taking the first sip of my drink, someone ran into me and made me spill my first sip on my top. I looked up to see a boy of my age stand startled in front of me.

"Oh I am so sorry. I didn't see you coming." He apologetically took out a tissue from his pocket and started wiping my top.

"Your eyes sticking up your ass or what?!" Silence followed my shout and then the boy broke it with his giggle. "You must be an A-lister dude," he said. I was frozen for a moment. How can a random guy guess my past? I gave him a cold stare and stormed out of the cafe praying I will never see his face again.

3

Good morning!" I wished Poppy as I buckled myself up in her car. "Good morning, Ally!" She sounded very energetic. "I picked you up first so that I can show you where the rest of us live." She steered down into another block.

"Well that's a good idea."

Poppy picked Adrian and Lucy and in no time we were sitting at Cafe'o. It was a few blocks away from our school and was indeed a nice place to hang out with friends. The place was brightly lit with low hanging lights and beautiful wallpapers supported the delightful ambience. The place was lined up with wooden chairs and tables which were decorated with flowers at the edges for delivering a unique look. I bought myself a cheese sandwich accompanied with a large cup of coffee and then joined the rest of the group at a corner table.

"So Adrian, where are you planning to take Poppy this year?" Lucy asked as she took a bite from her cheesecake gateau.

"What's the occasion?" I asked excitedly. "Well, you see Alina," Lucy explained, "It's their anniversary and every year Adrian takes me and Poppy to amusement parks and other fun places for a friends' day out."

"A friends' day out on an anniversary? Well that sounds really good," I smiled at Poppy as she again started to turn beet red. Adrian got up from his chair and announced out loud, "Ahem. Well my dear friends, this year we are going to hit the carnivals as it happens only once every two years and Ally Tally, you are gonna come with us. No questions asked."

"And when is this?"

"12th of August," Adrian sat back. The date rang in my ears. It was my dad's birthday. The fact that it would be his first birthday without him hit me hard and I somehow kept my feelings suppressed. "Guys I am really sorry but my mom wants me to go with her somewhere on the 12th. You guys go on, I will join in next time."

"Come on Ally, just postpone the thing with your mom," Poppy protested.

"Guys trust me, if it were possible, I would have come." And then no one asked me any more questions.

The first bell had already rang when we entered the school so I hurried to my English class and took the seat at the back again. The final bell rang and all the students came in, claiming their seats around the class. The teacher entered as everyone was settling down and that's when a familiar voice called out to me, "Hi." I turned beside and saw a tall figure standing near me. It was the boy who ran into me the day before.

Is he here to tell me that I was rude?

"Hi," I said in a low tone. "Please settle down," the teacher ordered and he sat beside me.

"What's your name?" He almost whispered. "Er... I am Alina," I replied, still hesitating and wondering what would come up next. He was about to say something but was interrupted by the sharp call of the teacher. "Alina, you and Liam Ivoshkov are paired for this semester. For everybody else as well, the partners won't be changed anymore for this semester." And then she started taking out some chits from her backpack. "Wow. Now I am paired with someone I don't even know. And who's this Liam anyways? Hadn't even seen him," I wondered out loud.

"I am Liam." The boy replied, rattling my nerves. "Oh." I hardly heard my voice. Then I gained some strength and spoke again, "Well. Seems like we have to be a team, Liam."

"Indeed," he scoffed.

"Alright pick a chit." The teacher announced and everyone went over to her desk to pick up one chit each. I collected mine and as I sat back, I opened it. It read 'Love'.

"Love. Hmm." I turned to Liam. "What have you got?"

"Hope," he laughed.

Love and hope? How am I gonna write anything on these two words when the only person I loved has left this world and I am left with no more hope? Irony does taste bitter eh?

"Now your assignment is to write an essay on the words you have got in your chits. The word limit is 2000." The teacher announced and I sat quietly in confusion and pain.

Liam said he did not believe in love as well. "But hope? I think I can write something up on that. At Least I am hoping so." And then he laughed again. "Can I get your number anyways?" He added.

"Huh? Yeah sure." I wrote my number on the back of his chit and handed it back to him. He looked at the chit and smiled. "Well I did hope I can get your number." I rolled my eyes, "You are ruining your own joke."

"My bad," he said and started to walk away. "See you later Alina."

Well I hope... ugh! Nevermind.

The doorbell rang over and over again, forcing me to cover my ears with the pillow.

I wish the person realises how early it is to ring someone's bell and walk away, or atleast, Mom, open up the goddamn door!

But nothing happened. I got up and stormed towards the main door. I took a glance at the clock. It was five in the morning, and that just aroused my anger.

I pulled open the door with a jerk and roared at the visitor, "What?!" And then I realised it was none other than Liam. "Did I wake you up?" He said gently and delivered a smile that blew away all my anger. But my annoyance stayed. "What on earth are you doing here at 5 in the morning?" He gave me a nudge and entered inside. "Well the assignment is due three weeks. So I thought maybe we can do some brainstorming and hunt some ideas. How about we go out for a fresh perspective?"

"Yeah Liam, we can go out and thank you for reminding me about the assignment," I clenched my teeth in anger and continued, "But this still doesn't explain waking somebody up at five in the morning! Or does it?"

"Well I can explain that if you go up, get dressed and let me take you somewhere." He stood with his hands crossed, waiting for my reply.

"Fine." I said and walked upstairs to get changed. "And I will make myself feel at home. Thank you!" He said sarcastically and sat on a couch.

I came down to see Liam engrossed in one of the books Dad used to read. "Come on," I said, pulling the book away from him. And then I remembered. "Oh wait. Let me tell Mom that I am leaving," I started walking back upstairs when I heard him call from behind. "Ahem. I have left for America and will be back soon. Love, Mom." I turned back. He was holding a note in his hand.

Why would Mom leave for America?

I locked the house and headed towards Liam's car. Halfway down the driveway I stopped and looked at the car blankly. It was a Ferrari Roma, the beast I was about to buy before my life turned upside down. It was the first thing I dreamt of having and then couldn't. It was the point of turn. "Come on, get in!" Liam honked the car twice, pulling me back to the present. I got in with a faint smile and buckled up. "Ready?" He turned on the ignition. "Yes." And we took off.

After driving for about 30 minutes, we finally stopped. I looked around. Dense forest stretched on either side and the road below was covered in dry leaves. "What are we even doing here? Are you gonna murder and dump me for what I did in Starbucks?" I chuckled. "Just follow me and I promise it will be worth it. And no one's murdering you for whatever happened at Starbucks. I am not angry for that. Rather I would say I am impressed." And he walked into the forest.

Well that compliment felt embarrassing in a good way.

We walked for about ten minutes before we reached an open field with an overgrown patch of stinging nettles. "Thank God, I wore a full pair of jeans." I said as I walked through the nettles. "Yeah they can be stingy enough to bring up rashes. Watch your step." Liam kept walking straight and when I was about to be fed up from all that walking, he stopped. I walked up to him and looked ahead. The empty sky with a tint of orange stretched far ahead of us, and the wind seemed to push us ahead. "It will be here any minute now," Liam announced. I stood there, looking at the sky, and then suddenly I felt Liam's chin touch my shoulder. His cheek rubbed against mine and I could hear his soft breathing. He placed his hand on my shoulder and I felt a blush creep up its way on my cheeks. It all made my spine shiver and then he raised his finger to point at the sky and said, "Look, there it is."

I looked up to see the sun slowly rising from behind the ridges. It brightened up the sky slowly and the dull red ball started shining on the fields, making the wildflowers steal its colours and bloom. It was all so magnificent. I had never seen anything like this before. The wilderness had not attracted me enough until that day. And then I heard Liam whisper, "Hope." I looked at him. He was so close. "The sun rises with new hopes of a new day. It tells us that the night, which is now left behind, has taken away all our bad memories and that now, it's time to make some new ones."

"Wow." I gave away a broad smile. "See, I told you, I have a few ideas. And that now, my knock at five in the morning, has been explained well enough, let's go grab something to eat." I nodded and followed him to his car.

When we came back to his car, I was still mesmerized by what happened earlier and a faint smile hung on my lips. "When did you buy this car?" I asked him as he started getting in.

"It's a birthday present from my mom."

"It's a nice one."

"Yeah it is," he held the steering and smiled.

"So, do you race?"

Why did I even ask that?

"Where did that come from?" He giggled. "But anyways, you are talking to a pro here. I race a lot, I win a lot."

"Good for you."

"Tell me. Do you race? Oh I am sorry.. eh.. do girls race?" He raised an eyebrow. I smiled at his competitiveness and replied, "Are you challenging me?"

"Well last time a girl said that, she lost." He chuckled softly. It was enough to put my ego on fire. "Very well then. We will race. And if I win, you will give me a ride, to and from school for a month."

Did I really place a challenge?

"Cool. And If I win, you are coming to the carnival with me." That took me back for a moment. But then again, I was too excited to think about it. "Done."

"Well then, give it a try. He tossed the car key at me. I grabbed it, got in and buckled up. "So should we go through the basics?" He said sarcastically. "Oh don't you worry about the basics." I turned on the ignition and in a moment we were gliding on the main roads. The 7 am traffic hustle had just pushed in, but nothing seemed to slow me down. I zipped my way through the speeding vehicles and stayed focused on the road. "You are good at it." Liam said as he tightened his seat belt. I could sense his nervousness. "Well, the best part remains." I said and pushed hard on the metal and continued, "Do you see those two trailers ahead?" He nodded. "What about that?" He held onto the seat belt harder.

"Well the one behind is gonna overtake the other before the next turn. And we, my friend, are gonna overtake them both."

"Uh huh. Uh huh." He replied and then as he realized what I was about to do, his face went pale. "No. No. No. Alina you can't do that."

"Oh, I can."

"What I mean is you shouldn't do that!" He was done acting strong. He could now sense the fear. But I felt different. I felt calm. I felt confident. So I pushed ahead, and as the trailer overtook the other halfway, I saw the gap in between and knew it was my opportunity.

"Alina, you are a great racer. I agree! Now just stop!"

But I was too confident to hear his advice. And before the trailer could overtake and cross the one ahead, I zoomed off from between, leaving the trailers behind and Liam in shock. For a few seconds he stayed frozen. And then he burst out, "That was crazy! That was just crazy! How did you pull that out! Oh my God that was so damn crazy! You are crazy!"

I kept laughing at his pale face. "I thought you were used to these things."

"Used to it? I am not used to madness! One mistake and we could have ended like canned sardines!"

God he almost lost his goddamn mind.

"Have you done that before?"

"No."

"Then how on earth did you do that now? How were you so confident?!"

"I was not."

"Then how?!"

"Hope." I smiled at him. He looked at me with blank eyes, slowly gaining back his breath.

We had breakfast at a cafe and then he dropped me back home. He swore to not let me drive ever again, to which I giggled heartily. "Thank you for today." I turned back to him and said. "Oh you are welcome! Now tell me. What are we going to about love?" He asked.

"Huh?"

"The second chit, Alina. Love."

"Oh! Yeah I will think about it."

God, where did my mind slip on that?

"Well, so will I," he said and took off. I stood there, gazing at the trail of dirt, and thinking what that new feeling inside me was.

God, it's tickling my stomach. What is it? Is it love? Nah. It's definitely the other one. Hope.

4

After the extraordinary morning with Liam, I was very exhausted.

A small nap will help me out.

And then I dozed off until my phone rang in my ears. It was Adrian.

"Al. Where are you?"

"Where will I be this early Adrian? I am at home. Sleeping."

"Early? Sleeping? Do you know what time it is?" He sounded a bit surprised. I was drowsy enough to pay attention to his useless blabbers. "10 AM I guess."

"Oh I see, Al. You have lost the sense of time." His laugh sounded irritating over the speaker. "And why so?" I opened my eyes.

"Why? Okay let's see. Maybe because it's 6 PM you sloth!"

I jumped out of the bed and looked at the screen - my vision still blurred with accumulated rheum. Adrian was right. I slept all day. "Anyways. Why did you call me?" I asked, trying to deviate from the topic.

"Well I was just asking whether you will join us for dinner or not?"

I succeeded.

"No Adrian. I have a lot of homework to do. You guys go on."

"Come on. It's a Saturday night."

"Well no. Don't bug me anymore."

And I disconnected. I knew I sounded rude, but I didn't feel like going out after Dad passed away. Everytime I woke up, his memories would hit my mind, and I would feel a sharp pain in my heart realizing the fact over and over that I won't see him ever again.

The only good thing I ever had, lasted less than it was meant too.

I went down to grab a bite when I remembered I haven't talked to my friends back in America since I shifted to London.

It's time to call Jessica.

I dialled her number and waited. The dial tone started getting on my nerves and when I thought she wouldn't pick up - she did.

"Hello?"

"Hey Jess! It's me, Al. How are you holding up?"

"Oh! Hi Al! I am fine. Do you need anything?"

Well that sounded weird and hurt a lot.

"Oh no. Nothing. I just called to check out on you guys. So how's everyone holding up?" I tried to sound normal.

"Yes Al, we are all fine here. Tell me about you. How are you and your mom managing? I heard you lost all the properties and the company as well."

Well that sounded like pity and I hate pity.

"Yeah Jess, Mom's fine. So I was saying…"

"Well that's good Al!" She interrupted. "Well listen, I have some work to do so I will catch you later. Bye." And she hung up.

Well I hate that too.

Tears rolled down my cheeks as I realized the harsh reality of friendship. It lasts only till you stand up to their expectations. I wiped my tears, took the car keys and went out.

I drove for two long hours but couldn't sooth myself down. Nothing seemed enough to forget what had just happened. I steered left and came down the highway to go to the one place I treasured the most. It was a lake with a huge oak tree that stood firmly, always waiting to welcome the visitors. The night sky was lit with stars and the cool breeze under the oak tree made me calm.

At last something calmed me down.

My dad had taken me there for the first time on my thirteenth birthday. It was one of the places he cherished the most. "Alina do you see the oak tree?" He pointed at it back then and I nodded in amusement. "Well every time I am sad, I come down here, look at the countless stars, and take a deep breath to fill myself with this sweet air. Then I tell the tree about my problems and tie a string around it."

"And does it make you feel better?"

"Well yes, it helps me out. Next time you are sad, try it out."

And there I was, standing under the tree without him. I sat there for a couple of hours, staring at the tree. Then I got up and tied an orange string around it. There were some old strings tied to the tree. I smiled at them as I tied mine. And then I noticed something. There was a zip lock bag tied to one of the old strings. I removed it and opened the bag. An old and crumpled piece of paper lied inside it. It was a note left by dad. My hands shivered as I unfolded it to read.

Al. If you are reading this, then I know you must be feeling lonely or lost. You are here to deal it my way though! Well I am sorry that I am not there at the moment to hear your problems. I might be busy with my stupid business. But when I get back, we will talk about you. I will always be with you, Al.

Love, Dad.

I went back to my car and drove back home. A smile pinned to my face and a new hope sparkling within me.

Back at home, I saw Mom busy in the kitchen. "Hi Sweetie! How was your day?"

"So you are back, huh?" I ran to her and hugged her from behind.

Sometimes, I just love that lady!

5

That Sunday I informed Adrian that I won't be needing a ride on Monday. Afterall, Liam had agreed on picking me up for school.

I slowly got up from my bed the next day as Liam said he will come within an hour. After a long shower I went down for breakfast.

"Good morning honey!" My mother wished me heartily. "There's milk in the fridge and a packet of cereal in the cupboard. Can you grab it for yourself?"

"Yeah sure. Thanks." I smiled.

A perfect morning after a long time.

I was busy with the dishes after breakfast, when I heard the doorbell ring. It was Liam. I rinsed quickly, grabbed my bag and left bidding goodbye to mom.

"Well someone is looking good today." Liam complemented as we walked through the driveway.

"Well thanks."

Did I just blush?

And then my eyes fell on his car. He has brought a Lamborghini that made me squeal with joy. "Can I drive?" I protested.

"Yeah in your dreams." He scoffed. "I am not letting you drive ever again Al, not even if it's your car."

"Fine." I growled and sat in the passenger seat.

After driving in silence for a couple of minutes Liam finally decided to speak. "So Al, what are you doing today after school?"

"Nothing much. Why?"

"Well because I am planning to take you somewhere."

"Not a jungle again eh?" I laughed awkwardly.

"No. Not a jungle." He laughed. "Then what Liam?" I wondered out loud to which he smiled, "You will see."

We stopped near school, and started getting out. "Al, meet me here at the parking lot after school." Liam instructed. I nodded to that and we went our separate ways.

The first half passed away smoothly and then after lunch I dragged myself towards the Chemistry class. Adrian sat beside me. His broad smile indicated he wanted to mock me. And then he did, "So I heard that you went out with Liam. No wonder you didn't carpool with us." I rolled my eyes and replied, "It's nothing like that. He came by at 5 yesterday morning out of the blues, and did the same today. It's not like I had a choice." Adrian's smile broadened at my statement, and then he let his dirty thoughts out, "And what were you guys doing so early eh? Physical workout?" I realised what he meant and smacked him. But after a few more mockings and repeated questions I gave up and told him everything.

He is a good listener. I can say that for sure.

"Al, that sounds like a good experience!" He chimed. I laughed heartily, "I know right?" And time flew away like always.

I couldn't control my excitement as I hurried down the corridor and stepped outside in the parking space finally. I made my way to Liam's car and then stood there blankly. He was not around, so I decided to wait. And then he sprang from behind the car, "Hi!" I was completely startled and shook to my core. That made all my emotions erupt, "Don't ever sneak on me like that again!" Liam had shown me so many colours of life in the last few days. And his weird humour had nurtured the child inside me, even though I would never admit it in front of him.

"Yeah right." He stood there, imitating my expressions. "Tell me when you are done with that." I rolled my eyes and slipped in the front seat. "Alright, let's go." He got in and we took off. After a while he took the turn that leads to my home. "Woah. I thought you were taking me somewhere." I looked at him disappointedly. "Well yes I am. But I need you to pick up some clothes before we leave." He said, with his eyes still on the road. "But where are we going Liam?" I was getting desperate by every second. "Yeah trust me. I can't wait as well." He laughed. When we came to my place, he parked his car and we got down. "Ok you wait inside. I will go pack up." And then as I turned to walk away, he held my wrist gently, "No. I will help you to pack up. After all, I know where we are going."

Focus Al. He is just acting friendly. Don't let dirty thoughts cloud your mind.

"Earth to Alina!" Liam snapped his fingers in front of me. I realised I had been standing still for a long time. "Yeah." I regained my senses. "Come on then." And we walked in.

Liam's POV

Alina stared at me blankly, but she had an unusual spark in her eyes. I couldn't stare back at her as I felt a sudden urge within me that would bring no good. "Earth to Alina!" I finally blurted out, trying to break the silence. Alina was staring at me like she was going to eat me, those beautiful green eyes looking at me. She snapped out of her thoughts and then replied, "Yeah, come on in." And we walked ahead.

Her room was simple and elegant. It had a soft purple paint on the walls with French doors that led to a balcony and on one side a huge king-sized bed was placed with an off-white comforter. She led the way into a walk-in closet filled with fashionable casuals and bold attires. I was impressed. Two rows were filled with shoes and bags with various shades meant for different occasions. "Woah Al, are you a control freak?" I wondered out loud. "Not me. My mom does all this. She likes things organized." She replied with a sweet smile that has always made me feel better. The first time I saw her at Starbucks I was shocked because I had never seen a feisty girl like her before. Usually, girls around me act all stylish and try to gain my attention, and I hated it. But Alina was different. Instead of falling for my charms, she embarrassed me in the middle of a cafe. And weird but true, I liked it.

Hormones eh?

I thought I would never see her again but when I walked into the class that day and saw her sitting at the last bench, my heart skipped a beat. She looked like an angel dropped straight from the heavens. I had never fallen in love before, but this seemed a lot like it.

"Earth to Liam!" She snapped her fingers in front of my face. "Did you even hear what I just said?" I smiled in return and replied, "I am sorry. I was just thinking about something. What were you saying?"

"What clothes do you want me to pack?"

I took a glance at her collection and took out a pink sundress, a short sleeve top and a sleeveless evening dress and then turned to her, "Here. And don't forget to pack your swimsuit." She nodded and I left her alone to pack. "

Alina came down after a while with her bag. "I will call and tell mom about the trip." She said. "Yeah sure. Tell her we will be gone for two days." I replied. And she walked away to get her phone.

Alina's POV

"Yeah mom. I will call you everyday. Don't worry, I will be fine." I said and hung up the phone. Mom agreed for the trip so I locked up the front door and made my way to Liam's car outside. He had already loaded the bags and was talking to someone on the phone. "Ready?" He hung up the call and held the steering. "Yeah let's go." I nodded and we took off. We drove for an hour before I started losing my patience. "Are we there yet?" Liam could see my desperation. "No. Half an hour more."

And then it felt like a year passed away. I sat motionless for more than two hours and then was finally moved by the view of long beaches. We had come a long way from home.

Liam finally stopped the car in front of a hotel. We got down and went inside. The hotel was actually an exotic resort near the beach. With an elegant facade and a lobby decorated with flowers and antique furniture, the resort defined its uniqueness well enough. There were guests from all around the globe, praising the beauty and hospitality of the resort. "Hey Al." Liam called out from the reception. I had been sitting in the waiting area. "They need your ID for check in." I walked over to the desk and slid my passport over it. The receptionist scanned our IDs and gave Liam a card key. "We hope you enjoy your stay at

The Beach Side Resort, Mr. Ivoshkov." She smiled at us and continued, "Your luggage will be sent to your room after the security checks."

Why a single card key? Why on earth would he book a single room?

Once the bellboy delivered the luggage and left with a handsome tip and a broad smile, I decided to confront Liam. "Why one room Liam?" I asked.

"Huh?"

"You could have booked two suites. Couldn't you?"

"Actually no, Al. They had only one room left, and I was stuck with last moment reservations and couldn't find rooms nearby as well. We can manage, can't we?" He looked at me hopefully.

God I will never win against that stare.

"Fine. Just fine." I said and started walking out but then stopped near the gate and turned to him. "What?" He shrugged.

"You wanted to show this to me? A suite?" I raised an eyebrow. "Oh no Al." He smiled and continued, "Today we rest. Tomorrow it's going to be a long day."

"And?"

"And we see it tomorrow Al. Isn't it obvious enough?"

I walked away silently.

Nothing is obvious with you around, Liam.

6

The hotel suite was extraordinary but just like any other suite in that range. What made it beautiful and unique was Liam's presence. After having dinner and taking a hot shower, I went to the living room. "Al, put on something nice. I wanna show you something." Liam said and went outside.

Giving privacy before one demands it, makes you a true gentleman. I appreciate that Liam.

And with a broad smile I changed my clothes and went outside. Liam was already in his car, waiting for me at the portico. In a while we were on the road, taking our journey to another level.

After driving for about half an hour, Liam stopped in front of a cafe. I was mesmerized by the looks of it. The cafe was a small and comfortable one, situated right by the beach. One can sit there for hours and listen to the soothing waves crashing on the cold sands. The area around was not crowded as well, and was perfect for an evening walk along the beach. What made the cafe unique and distinguished was its structure. The cafe was actually carved out of a giant driftwood that had washed ashore long ago. It was one of the unique cafes that make it to the annual hospitality magazines. "This is one of my favourite places. Whenever I come here, I visit this cafe." We took a corner seat with a glass window beside. The furniture were all carved from wood and the ambience was soothing and refreshing. A faint smell of fancy incense sticks tickled my nose, and as I looked around, Liam tossed the menu card at me. "What will you have?"

"It's your place of choice. Why don't you suggest?" I tossed the card back. "Well, since we already had dinner let's just stick to the desserts eh? The sticky toffee pudding with vanilla ice cream is something you should try from here." He suggested. "Well alright." I nodded and he ordered two portions.

After he placed the orders we talked for a couple of minutes before I threw in a stupid question, "So Liam. Tell me about your love life. Do you have any girlfriends?"

"Why do you ask?" He raised an eyebrow as if mocking me. I scoffed, " You see, I don't want her to have any wrong intentions about us." He smirked at my nuisance, "You can have wrong intentions Alina. I don't have any girlfriend after all."

Did he just say I can have wrong intentions? Am I blushing?

And before I could reply our desserts arrived, and we dug in. The ice cream melted in my mouth and the soft crunch of the toffee made the pudding extremely satisfying. "I have had this pudding so many times, but I have to admit. This, right here, is the best." I said as I wiped cream off my lips. "Told you, it's good." Liam smiled politely. We laughed and teased over the pudding and before we knew, it was over. So after settling the bills, we stepped out and the ocean waves drew my attention instantly. "Can we go in the water?" I pleaded to which Liam nodded with a gentle smile.

I tossed my sandals and ran bare feet on the cool and wet sand. The waves came crashing at my feet and washed away the footprints that I left behind as I walked along the shore. I stopped and stared at the waves, as it washed away my prints on the sand and left the sand untouched once again. My psychiatrist has mentioned this phenomena a while ago and related this to life so well. *ever be a barrier that is between the foot imprinted in the sand in a beach and the water, because if you do so, the mark will never be erased. But if you step aside and let the water wash it away, then there will be no sign of it so you can go on creating new imprints. That is how the past and the future is to be handled., The past is the imprint and unless you forget that and move on, you can never create happiness in the future. Let the time act like water and wash away the painful past. And then you can find peace in the present, Al.*

"Al, are you listening ?" Liam asked me something but I didn't hear him. Sorry I wasn't listening. What did you say?" I asked. "Shall we make a sandcastle?" He asked. "That would be fun! Come on!" I said and we started working on it. When we were done, Liam took a picture of it and I was about to build one more tower when a huge wave came and washed away our castle. Liam pulled me away, saving me from getting wet. "Thanks. That was close." I giggled. After that we went back a few feet and sat down on the sand, looking at the waves. The sound of night was so serene and addicting. I closed my eyes and enjoyed the cold breeze touching my cheeks. It made my hair flutter and soon I started feeling cold. "Oh God, I should have brought a jacket with me." I mumbled and rubbed my palms. Suddenly, I felt a warm soft jacket drape around me and when I opened my eyes and looked at Liam, he delivered a smile. "Liam no, you will be feeling cold." I was about to give his jacket back when he placed his warm hands on my shoulder. "You were shivering. It's alright. Give it to me later." He said.

"Thank you!" I said and then looked above at the night sky. "The sky is so beautiful today. Look at the stars dancing around the moon. I wish I could be one of them, dancing around the moon." I wondered out loud. "You are the moon, Al. You don't need to dance around with the stars. You are the one who shines." Liam said, still looking at the stars. I smiled.

My dad always used to tell me the same thing.

"Why are you crying, Al? Is something wrong?" Liam asked me with concern.

Now when did I start to cry?

I quickly wiped my tears rolling down my cheeks and stood up. "I think it's the sand irritating my eyes." I said, brushing my clothes. "Shall we go back? I think it's getting late." He nodded and replied, "Yeah why not? Let's get back to the hotel." He took my hand in his, and we made our way back to his car .

"Liam, I thought the hotel was that way. I think we missed a turn." I told him as we drove through the silent roads. We had been driving for a few minutes, and I felt that we were going the wrong direction. "Don't worry, Al. I know the roads over here by heart, and we are heading to a last destination before we call it a night." He said, and after ten minutes of driving, we stopped near a small ice cream stall. "Let me get the door for you." Liam said and got down to open the door for me.

Damn, he's such a gentleman.

We made our way towards the ice cream stall. There were hardly any people around, and almost all the shops were closed. "Liam, it's past midnight and you want to have ice cream? That too after we have had our desserts?" I asked bewildered. "I have never done such crazy things in my life before. What's wrong with that? And it's not like you are diabetic. Come on, you have to try it for my sake, please." He insisted. "Fine. Let's go." I mumbled and followed him quietly.

He went to the ice cream vendor and got himself a peanut butter and vanilla ice cream. I ordered a double chocolate chip ice cream. When we got our ice creams, we made our way to a nearby bench and sat down to eat. "Hmm. This tastes so good. I can taste a bit of sea salt in it though." I said enjoying the flavour of the ice cream." I said.

"I told you it's going to be good, especially when you eat it at this time. And that salt you taste, is coming from your fingers that you can't stop licking." He chuckled.

We talked for a long time. I never realized how fast time flew away. "God Liam! It's almost three in the morning! Let's get back." I said and then we hurried back to the hotel. After freshening up, I sat by the mirror table and combed my hairs. After a few moments, the bathroom door opened and Liam came outside - half naked. I was taken aback and my face turned beet red. I wasn't sure if I felt awkward, angry, or shy. "Liam, I think you should put on a shirt."

"Nah, I am not comfortable sleeping that way." He said and before I could plead more, he jumped onto the bed. "You can't sleep on the bed with me." I said. "Well of course I can. And don't worry, I will not roll over you. And if you still feel uncomfortable, there are cushions on the sofa. "Lay them like a boundary in between, and you will be just fine." He said and I followed his instructions.

Just wanted to make sure, you know?

Liam's POV

The sun was shining brightly on my face when I woke up. I was about to get up and close the curtains when I felt something heavy on my chest. Al was sleeping peacefully, snuggling close to me. I smiled at her, and slowly placed her head on my pillow and moved out to go to the bathroom. I glanced at my phone. It was already past ten and that meant the breakfast buffet was already closed. So I decided to eat outside.

But then again, how could I wake her up, knowing she must be wandering peacefully in her dreams.

7

Alina's POV

After breakfast, we packed our things and went back home. "Thank you for the wonderful trip. I really enjoyed it."

"You're welcome, Al. I am glad you enjoyed your time." Liam said and with that I took my bags, got out of the car and made my way to the front porch. When I was about to knock the door, it flew open and my mom came out. She hugged me and whispered near my ears, "Oh Alina! Welcome home. I missed you so much." "I missed you too mom." I replied and we went in. As I closed the door, I searched around for Liam, hoping to see him leave but he was already gone.

"So Alina, tell me about your trip."

"Oh it was great mom. I had a great time!"

"Well I can see that in your face."

"What do you mean?"

"You are smiling. After a long time, I would say." She replied with moist eyes. I hugged her in silence.

"Good morning, Al. So how was your getaway? Was it fun?" Lucy bombarded me with her questions when I got into her car the next morning. "Well it was great. Let's talk all about it at lunch alright?" "Cool." She said and we drove to the school.

"Hey Ally!" Adrian came running at me as I walked into the school corridor. He seemed so excited.

Now it's his turn to bombard me eh?

And then he asked tons of questions in one breath. Most of them I wasn't sure if I could answer. "Don't worry Ally Tally. We can talk about it over lunch.

Great.

"So Al, are you coming over with us for the fund raising event?" Poppy asked me as she joined us at the next turn. "Well… I…" And before I could finish Adrian jumped in, "Well of course she is coming! She owes us for not joining us on Saturday night."

"But Adrian, I have…"

"This conversation is over, Ally. You are coming with us and there is no room for argument." Adrian said to which I simply sighed. "Fine, count me in."

I had English in the first period. By the time I went inside the class, it was almost full and the last bell had already rung so I quickly made my way to the regular back seat. "Good morning, Al. Did you sleep well yesterday?" Liam whispered from beside. "Yes. And why do you ask?" I looked at him.

"Nothing specific." He smiled. The class had already begun. The teacher raised her voice and the class dropped into silence, "So students, I hope you are doing well with your assignments so far. Well today I wanted to tell you that this Friday will be a holiday and so I will be adding up an activity with your assignment." Everybody groaned at her announcement but she continued at the same tone, "I want you all to visit public places like cafes and shopping malls to ask people around about their opinion on the words you have. Any question?" Everybody started to mumble complaints and tried to push in some questions but she had already made herself clear. "So no questions then. Good." And she turned towards the blackboard. "Well then I will pick you up on Friday." Liam declared. I nodded with a long sigh.

During the lunch break, I thought of asking my friends about their opinion on the words I had for assignment.

Let's see what they have to say about love and hope.

I waited for a couple of minutes on our usual table for them to arrive, and then I encountered someone uninvited. She was a blonde, wearing high heels and by the time I realised she was coming towards me, she had already stopped in front of me. Her hands rested on her waist and she leaned onto one side, as if dominating the conversation she was about to start. "Can I speak to you for a minute?" She asked sharply. "Yeah, why not?" I said, trying to keep it cool.

"Look. I will get straight to the point. Stay clear of Liam. He's not your type and don't even try to seduce him into liking you. I know how to deal with the likes of you." She said as if spitting venom at me.

Woah there! You are messing up with the wrong girl bitch!

I gave her a dead glare, "Well if you want him so bad, why don't you just drag her all around. I don't have any feelings for him whatsoever, and we are just working together on an assignment."

"Well then it better stay that way! Don't make it a habit eh?" And with that, she stormed away. Lucy, Adrian, and Poppy were watching this from a few feet away, and as soon as she left, they dropped in. "What was that about?" Adrian asked me. "Well I don't know! She warned me to stay clear of Liam. I don't even have feelings for that guy. What a nutcase!" I shouted hoping she could hear me from across the corridor. Poppy waved her hands frantically in front of me, "Shush Alina! She is Liam's ex, Shelly. Maybe she's just jealous."

"Yeah then go on and shush her Poppy! No one has ever talked to me that way. Ever!" I said furiously. "Al, now come on! Just forget it. Let's talk about some pleasant stuff." Lucy said, trying to cheer me up.

That's right. Anger is bad Alina. Breath in, breath out.

"So guys, I want your help in my assignment." I opened up, trying to blow away the sudden tension. "Tell us. We are in." Poppy chimed. "Ok! So I want your opinions on the word, love." I asked and looked at their thoughtful faces.

"Well, for me, it's a feeling you get when you find your soulmate. It doesn't occur with any random person, but once you fall in love it's like you have successfully filled your life with colours and you won't feel lonely anymore." Adrian said with a polite smile. "Wow. That was good. Your turn Poppy!" I pointed my pen at her.

Oh me! For me love means care and happiness. You know that feeling when you believe something is really important? Like when you are around the person you really love, you feel butterflies in your stomach. And no matter how horrible that person is, you will always be able to see his true beauty." She said blushing. "So am i horrible Poppy?" Adrian asked doubtfully. "Well how can I tell? I love you remember?" Poppy giggled.

"Well that was deep. Your turn Lucy." I gave her a smile to which she delivered a wise expression. "Hmm. Let me think. I have never fallen in love before, but I can tell the people I would call love are my friends. They have always been there for me and I will be there for them always. We have no secrets among us and that measures our closeness well enough. So for me, love is nothing but a bond. A bond that is not visible through naked eyes, but you can feel it when you are around the people you share it with. Just like I feel it now."

Okay. That was emotional.

"Damn, I love you guys so much. Don't leave my side ever you ugly mud balls!" She laughed but had tears in her eyes. We all hugged each other laughing and then walked out.

For me? Well for me, love is a feeling that has a different meaning in every individual's life. And you fall for the one, whose meaning for love exactly defines your existence!

8

Friday mornings were not always so relaxing. The unexpected holidays just made them soothing. I was so happy.

Time to find mom and have some warm breakfast.

"Alina, I had some urgent business to deal with in America, so I came here yesterday. I will be back in two days. Can you stay alone at home or should I ask my friend Michelle to come over and stay with you?" Said my mom when I called her after going around the house like a dozen times.

"No mom. I think I can handle two days. You take care." I told her and placed the receiver back.

I decided to cook myself some breakfast, but the doorbell interrupted. I opened the door to see Liam stand outside with a takeaway box.

"Hey Al!" He said and entered inside. "I thought maybe I will have my breakfast today with you and your mom. So I brought some food if that's okay." I rolled my eyes and let out a sigh, " Well mom's not home. She has gone to America and will return in two days." He seemed lost for a moment and then he replied, "Very well then. We can have breakfast together perhaps. And hey, I am home alone too! Why don't we stay together at my place?" I scoffed sarcastically and said, "Well no. I don't think so." He was taken aback, as if I denied him his basic right. "Why? Aren't we friends?"

"No, Liam. We are not friends. We are just together in an assignment and once I am done with it, I am done with you." I gave him a cold stare. "And may I ask why?" He questioned politely.

I didn't know what to say. My annoyance was clouding my thought process, but then I finally replied, "You are one of those A-listers and I don't want to be associated with you or get involved with stupid fights because of you." He seemed a bit unsure of what I said. "Al, just because I am one of the elite ones doesn't mean I can't be friends with you. What's wrong with you Al?" He sounded angry. "Look." I replied, trying to hide my emotions, "Let's just finish the assignment and then we won't have to argue anymore." With that I strided outside. "Fine. Get in the car and we can go for that activity." He instructed loudly and I sat in his car without uttering a word.

After what felt like eternity we finally reached a small cafe. It was bustling at that time of the day, so we went in and started our activity of gathering public opinion for the two designated words. I approached a middle-aged woman and introduced myself. She was really sweet and when I told her about my work, she willingly accepted to help. "So what is your opinion about hope ma'am?" I asked her. She said hope was something her career has always relied on. She mentioned how she became a successful managing director in one of the leading companies in London, although she had started only as a regular tenant in small companies. I got acquainted with many others who shared their own opinions and experiences about hope and then I went back to Liam's car after I was done with my part. A few minutes passed away and then Liam came. He handed me a few sheets and got in his car without speaking a single sentence. We drove back as silently as we came. I got out of the car when we reached my house, and then turned back to thank him but he drove away before I could let out a word.

I was busy preparing myself dinner late that night, when I heard the bell ring. I opened the door to see Adrian standing at the door.

"Hey Ally Tally! Put up your shoes and come with me." He said excitedly.

"And where are we going exactly?" I demanded.

"Well it's a Friday night out, and you cannot deny it because you already owe us a lot of cancelled plans already." He concluded. "Fine." I said and went in to get changed.

And then after a while there I was, sitting in Adrian's car, wondering about Liam and all that happened in morning.

It was hard to push him away, but that did save me from a heartbreak in future. Didn't it?

"Alright! We are here." Adrian announced, popping my thought balloon filled with bad thoughts. I looked at the club and sighed heavily. It was meant for people with money and reputation, and to be more specific, nothing new for me.

"Well I was right. Only Adrian can pull you out of that house of yours." Poppy giggled as we joined her and Lucy after a while. We ordered our dinner and soon were busy with cutleries and conversations. And then somebody interrupted. It was a tall guy with messy brown hair, and blue eyes. Adrian noticed him standing beside him and got up with open arms to exchange a warm hug. "Hey Adrian. How are you doing?" He asked and then turned to us. "Well hello ladies, and who's this beautiful one?"

I blushed awkwardly and decided to keep quiet. "That's Alina. She just moved from America." Lucy introduced me. "Alina, this is Luke Mellin. He used to study with us, before he shifted to a different one."

"Nice to meet you Alina." He shook hands with me and we exchanged smiles. "So Alina, can i have a dance with you?" He asked and stood there smiling.

Well it was sudden. And I didn't know if it would be ok to deny. So I accepted.

When we were on the dance floor, the song changed and this time it was a slow one. Luke held me closer, and we started swaying with the music. It was all good, and I was actually enjoying it, but then I spotted Liam. He stared at me from the corner of the room. I quickly looked away and ignored him as he was not there. "Maybe you can come to the fund-raising event, and we will get to know each other better." Luke said. "Sure." I replied with a smile, trying to forget the fact that Liam was staring at me.

We came back home before midnight, and after taking a nice long shower, I decided to go to bed. But then my phone chimed. It was Liam's text. 'Al. we need to talk.' And then another dropped in. 'I think you should stay away from Luke.' I rolled my eyes and kept my phone back.

His ex asked me to stay away from him. Now he is asking me to stay away from Luke. What am I? A puppet pulled by strings? Or just a string pulled by everybody?

9

The morning sun kissed my skin with its warmth. I opened my eyes and looked at my phone.

12 missed calls from Poppy. Wow.

And then it rang again, as if she never stopped calling. "Hey Al! Where are you?" She said as soon as I picked up. "Well. Sleeping." I replied and stretched myself. "When will you come to the park?" She questioned giggling. I took a look at my watch and replied, "Well around 10 I suppose." "Okay. I will be waiting." She said and disconnected.

See you Poppy. Bye.

After a few rolls back and forth, I finally got out of the bed and headed towards the bathroom. After having a nice shower, I ate a hearty breakfast and walked out.

I somehow expected it before but wasn't so sure until I saw Liam actually standing next to my car. He looked at me all confused and annoyed.

God how long has he been waiting there?

"Al, why are you doing this to me?" He questioned desperately as I entered my car and slammed the door shut. "Why are you acting so cold?"

"Maybe because I prefer staying this way" I replied with a sharp glare.

"What did I do to be treated this way Al?" He sounded worried now. "Look, Liam. Your ex or maybe your current, I really don't care, asked me to stay away from you so that is exactly what I intend to do from now on. Got it?" I replied to him harshly and took off. But that was not all that Liam had done. There was more.

Flashback

"And then we had ice-cream at the middle of the night. Can you guys believe it?!" I giggled after sharing every inch of details from the crazy night I had with Liam. But for some reasons Lucy seemed uncomfortable. "Al, I think I need to tell you something." She finally talked.

"Yeah Lucy. What is it?" I asked puzzled. "I think Liam is just playing around with you. You should not fall for him I would suggest." She said and Adrian and Lucy agreed. "Yeah actually we didn't feel like telling it to you until now. Look, we have seen him break so many hearts. He is just a guy fooling around with others' emotions." Adrian said, trying to keep his voice low. I laughed nervously, "I don't think he is like that at all. There might be a misunderstanding."

"He dated me too Al." Lucy confessed and silence covered us all. "He dated me for four months and then Shelly came up, so he dumped me. When I asked him the reason for it, he said he never had feelings for me." Tears started rolling down her cheeks as she finished speaking. I went over to her and hugged her tight, "Don't cry Lucy. It will be Okay." Adrian and Poppy consoled her as well. I had a perception that Liam might be different from other rih boys, but I was wrong. So I decided not to talk to Liam ever again and stay away from him as far as possible.

Flashback Ends

Liam called me from behind but I kept on driving. I looked at my rear-view mirror. He stood at the middle of the road, still looking at me. But I didn't stop.

The parking space around the park was almost full. I had a hard time finding a good place to park but then I finally found one.

"Sorry for being late guys. Had some issues to handle." I told my friends as I joined them inside. "That's alright. Can you handle the cash while I hand over the desserts?" Poppy asked and I nodded. "Sounds fun"

We stood in the sun and sold desserts for three hours straight. We had earned a lot of profit and the event was a complete success. "Now this calls for a celebration." Adrian announced as he peeled out tapes from his skin. He was covered in tapes as he was packing the desserts. We started walking out and that's when Luke came. "I am so sorry guys, I couldn't make it in time. I had to hit the airport to pick up my mom." He apologized. "That's alright Luke. Come on, join us for the celebration. Adrian says, there's an Italian restaurant nearby." Lucy invited her gracefully. "Sounds great." And he joined.

The restaurant was a ten-minute drive. We sat down and ordered our food in a while. The guys were excited about the Winter Ball. It was some kind of annual ball dance the students in the locality were crazy about the whole year. "I am going solo this year. Maybe I will find someone to dance with that night itself." Lucy announced and then turned to me. "What about you Al?" I wondered for a moment and before I could say I planned on going solo as well Poppy interrupted, "You don't have to go solo Al. You can go with luke. He is a great dancer.

Aren't you Luke. He giggled, "Well yes I am. And I can go with Alina. What do you say Al?" I looked at him blankly. I didn't know what to say, but then somehow I stammered, "Well… I… I will let you know." He nodded with a smile and then the food arrived.

Am I blushing again?

Liam's POV

I stood at the middle of the road, looking Alina drive away. I was really annoyed by her behaviour, so I stormed back into the house and slammed the door behind me.

Al was acting way too weird around me. She was nothing like the other girls I had met. She was different and I really liked her. I knew she had found out about my dating life and that's why she was doing this to me. But I couldn't leave her. She was someone I had always dreamt of and searched for a long time. I couldn't let her go like the rest of my past. I had to hold onto her and I was way too determined to quit so soon. "I will prove my love and care to her and I will win her back." I promised out aloud. And then with uncountable thoughts of her, I drifted off to sleep before I could even realize.

10

Alina's POV

After the delicious meal at the Italian outlet, Luke announced he wanted to give us all an ice-cream treat. So we headed to a nearby parlour and got into a long queue. "Guys I will just use the washroom and come back." I said and left. When I returned, Luke was still standing aside, talking to someone over the phone. "Let's go and get you that ice-cream." He disconnected the call and said to me. "You didn't need to wait for me. Now you have to wait with me in the queue again." I replied looking at him all confused. "As if I didn't know that. now come on, the queue is going crazy." He scoffed and then went in, while I followed him to the queue.

He is a good guy eh?

After standing for about ten minutes, we finally got ourselves ice-cream. Then we headed upstairs to rejoin the group.

The place was too crowded to find anny seat. Poppy was sitting on Adrian's lap and Lucy somehow had found a seat for herself. After waiting for a while Luke finally got us two seats. Our ice-cream had already melted halfway.

After we licked on our ice-creams silently for a moment, Luke spoke up, "So, are you friends with Liam? Like I heard people talk about it."

"That's what people do anyways. We are not friends. We are just working together on an assignment together." I answered him coldly. "Well, that sounds fun." He replied smiling. There was silence again for a moment and then he spoke up again, "Look Al, I understand if you don't feel like going with me to the ball, but if you do, I will be very happy." I looked at him for a second and then replied with a genuine smile, "Let's go together." His facial expressions changed instantly, "Really Al? Wow this will be so great! So tell me. Do you have a dress for the ball?" I shook my head, "Not yet. But I will pick something up soon."
We changed the topic thereafter. He shared his hobbies with me and so did I. I let him lead the conversation because I didn't feel like blurting any truth about my pitiful life by mistake. "So, how many siblings do you have?" He asked me after a while. "I don't." I replied. "Now that is great. Unlike me of course, I have an elder brother." He said scratching his head. "I have always wanted an elder brother." I wondered out loud. He looked at me and laughed heartily, "Trust me, you are better alone. He is just two years older than me and is so annoying that I can't even describe."

We talked for a long time. The parlour was not so crowded anymore. Adrian and others had left an hour ago. I looked at the watch and gasped, "Oh it's six! I think I am late. Let's save some talk for later." With that I got up and so did he. "It was nice talking to you." He said and unexpectedly gave me a hug. I was taken aback for a second, but then I hugged him back.

Damn it has been a weird day.

I came home, prepared myself some dinner and went up to my room to change into my comfortable pyjamas.

As I walked down the stairs, the landline rang. "Campbell Residence." I said as I picked up the receiver. It was mom. She wanted me to attend a dinner with her the next week. "Who is it mom?" I asked. "It's one of my old school friends. I bumped into her today at the hotel I am staying at. She has invited us to a dinner party at their place and we are going. Get yourself something nice to wear alright?" She answered and then disconnected shortly.

I had my dinner soon after that and then I fell asleep on the living room couch. I couldn't tell when I exactly fell asleep, but then the phone rang again and I was startled. I couldn't remember how I ended up sleeping on the couch. The phone continued ringing in my ears. I got up somehow and reached out for it. It was Poppy. "Are you kidnapped or something? I called more than five times." She snapped at me as soon as I received the call. "I felt asleep Poppy, chill." I said, yawning out loud. "Yeah whatever." She continued, "Be ready at ten in the morning. We are going shopping for the Winter Ball. Luke will come and pick you up."

"But Poppy… I.."

"I don't want to hear anything. No excuses please. We are going and that's it." She said and disconnected.

Will my friends ever let me decide anything?

The next morning I was busy cooking myself a breakfast when Luke arrived. He was half an hour early so I invited him to eat with me. "No Al, I already had a bowl of cereal and an apple today morning. Thanks anyways." He denied politely. "Well you wouldn't survive with that the whole day. Especially when we are going shopping." I said sarcastically. He laughed hard and said, "I think I will be just fine." I nodded and replied, "Yeah right. But I am not asking for your consent. Get your ass over that table right now." He grinned awkwardly and took a seat finally.

After a while I joined him at the breakfast table. "Where did you learn to cook from, Al? This looks so great." He complimented enthusiastically. "Well my mom is a good cook. Didn't have to learn from elsewhere." I replied and took a bite off my toast. "Hmm. This really is good." I said out loud, chewing on the toast.

"Told you eh?"

We talked about a lot of things and then suddenly he asked me the most unwanted question, "So Alina. You never told me anything about your dad." I felt a weird numbness on my face. "Well, he flies a lot. And most of the time he is away from home." I lied. I didn't want him to know much about me for reasons unknown. "Tell me more about your new school, Luke." I steered away successfully from the topic.

When we were done eating, I washed the dishes and turned to him, "So, where are we going first?"

"It's a famous boutique in London. You will like it." He said and we headed to his car. Luke held the door for me and I couldn't help but give away a broad smile.

"Right on time Al. Come on, I have opted out some outfits." Poppy dragged me towards the changing room as soon as I entered the boutique. Adrian and Luke got busy talking and we started selecting from a dozen of clothes. "Where's Lucy?" I asked as I looked around. "Oh she's already in the changing room." Poppy replied, still looking at the dresses. "Here. Try these. And find some more if you want. I will go get changed." She handed me over a set and then walked away. I dropped it as soon as she left.

Sorry Poppy.

"Hello ma'am. Can I help you?" A staff approached me with a greeting smile. "Yeah can I get something not much shining and maybe laces." I demanded. She nodded and asked me to go to a dressing room. "Please wait there ma'am and I will bring in some of our best collections. I made my way to the dressing room and after a while she came with a portable garment rack filled with dresses hanging all around it. I picked up a peach dress and tried it on.

"So, what do you all think?" I asked as I walked out after changing. "Nah Al. The colour is too contrasting. Makes you look dull." Lucy said and Adrian smirked. "What are you laughing at?" I eyed him. "Nothing. I just like the cuts." I rolled my eyes and went back in. Then I picked up a pink dress with sleeves off the shoulder.

"Now this goes well on you." Poppy commented. Luke looked at me from top to bottom and smiled, "You look beautiful in it, Alina." I blushed noticeably and walked back into the dressing room. "I got one last dress to check." I said as I went away. Then I finally returned wearing a deep purple dress, with a single slit on the right leg that came up to my thigh. It had one of those heart shaped necklines and also a lot of ribbon laced into roses resting above my breast.

"This is perfect." Poppy squealed.

"You look gorgeous!" Lucy exclaimed

"I think this is the one." I went in and picked up another dress for the dinner next week. Then I settled the payments and soon we were out on the streets of London.

Luke dropped me home later that night. I had a strange feeling that someone was looking at us but I constantly ignored it. "Thanks Luke. I had fun today." I said to him and he nodded with a smile. We got out of the car and stood on my driveway staring at each other when he finally spoke. "Are you coming to the matches next week? i am playing."

"I am sorry Luke. I really want to come but I have a wedding to attend." I apologized. "Oh that's okay. Maybe you can come the week after."

I nodded gracefully. "Definitely." And then I saw behind him. Luke was standing on the other side of the road. I was right. He was staring at us for a long time. "Hey Al." He called out. Perhaps he noticed I saw him. He walked towards us and then stopped a few feet away. "I wanted to hand you these notes." He handed me over a file.

"Thanks Liam. And oh, by the way, this is Luke. And Luke, this is Alan." I introduced them to each other.

"Oh I know Luke." He said, giving him a cold stare.

"And I know Liam." Luke replied sharply.

I could actually feel the tension building up and then Liam spoke. "So Al. You found yourself a boyfriend huh?"

"She's just a friend Liam." Luke cleared out but Liam seemed hardly interested in what he had to say. He was looking straight into my eyes. "Al. We need to finish that assignment if you don't mind. Can we go in?" And before I could say anything Luke came over to me and gave a hug. Then he retreated to his car. "Goodnight Al. I will see you tomorrow. "Bye Luke." I said, looking at Liam furiously.

"What do you want Liam?" I asked Liam loudly, shutting the door behind me as we got inside the house. "I want you to stay away from Luke." He replied firmly. And that just raised my temper. "What made you think that you can decide that?" I gritted my teeth in anger. "I care about you Al." Liam said. "Says the person with a cold heart? Oh please Liam! I know what kind of person you are so just quit acting!" I crossed my hands angrily. "I have changed, Al. You have changed me. And I can't let you just walk away after everything."

"Nothing happened Liam. And nothing will ever happen." I said coldly and there was silence for a while.

"Maybe not today. Maybe not even tomorrow. But one day I will prove it to you that I am a better person now. Goodnight Al. Take care." Liam replied and with moist eyes, he walked out. I came back to my bedroom and surprisingly started crying. I didn't know the reason, but I felt hurt and alone.

Not everything that hurts makes you cry. Not until it hurts you over and over.

11

FIVE DAYS LATER

The day arrived when we had to attend the dinner party. Mom was all excited and hurried down the hall as we left for the salon and spa appointments.

You don't want to attend these parties without a proper massage including manicures and pedicures and a nice haircut with some makeup.

We finally returned home around five in the evening. I put up the red dress I got myself last week for the party and walked downstairs. "Shall we go mom?" I said as I approached her. She was already waiting at the gate impatiently, but then she turned towards me and her face lit up with happiness. "Oh sweety, you look so beautiful." And then we left after exchanging some more compliments.

Her friend's house was no ordinary. It was huge to begin with and had a modern look mixed with a touch of the Victorian style. I was lost in its beauty but then my mom caught my attention by introducing me to the host. Her friend, Rose. She was a lady with long chocolate brown hairs, and a pair of beautiful eyes that seemed way too familiar. "Hello Alina." She held onto my hands and greeted me with a polite smile. "Hello, Miss Rose. It's a pleasure to meet you." I replied. "Ah please

Alina, just call me Rose. And the pleasure is all mine." She said gracefully and then led us inside.

Soon they got busy talking and I started texting Poppy. She was enquiring if I found somebody interesting over there. 'I don't visit places to find myself a boyfriend Poppy.' I texted her back and she just spammed my inbox with emojis.

After a while, somebody came walking downstairs. I could see a figure from the corner of my eyes but didn't bother to look away from my screen. "Alina, meet my son. Liam." She said and I froze for a second. As I looked up, Liam stood there with his hand stretched to shake mine. "Hello Alina. Nice to meet you." I shook his hands, forcing a smile on my face. He acted as if he never met me before.

"Liam, maybe you can take Alina and show her around." His mother suggested and he agreed. Soon we were out in the garden, walking quietly. And after a moment I spoke, "Why didn't you ever tell me that my mom was a friend of yours?" Liam scoffed sarcastically, "Yeah. As if I knew."

I believe him. I never asked him about his mother before anyways.

"Now. Come on. Let me show you around, eh?" He said and pulled me back inside. We walked upstairs and then headed down the corridor. It was well lit and the walls were full of splendid framed paintings. And then we stopped near a huge door. He opened it and stood aside, gesturing for me to step inside. I went in and looked around. Huge wooden bookshelves stood on all four corners of the room. There were innumerable books, waiting on the racks to be opened and explored. The pleasant smell from the books filled the room and I inhaled in deeply. It all reminded me of my dad's library back in America. It was one of my favourite places and whenever my mind craved for some peace, I used to sit there for hours. I was happy to see one again, and partly annoyed realising the fact that Liam knew my weakness and brought me inside on purpose.

I ran my fingers along the book spines and embraced the nostalgic feeling arousing within me. "There's something more I want you to see." Liam said and opened a French door at the far end of the room. I walked in with no other choice left. It was a conservatory filled with various plants resting on hanging pots. The room was plated with glass and a huge crystal chandelier right in the middle of the room illuminated every corner of it. The music from downstairs was audible in this room, unlike the library. "Shall we dance Al?" Liam asked, offering me his hand to hold onto.

I don't know...

"Well, what's the harm in that?" I smiled at him and he pulled me close to him, gently. He placed his hands on my waist and I felt heat rundown my spine. My heart raced and I felt goosebumps on my neck. But then I ignored my feelings and snaked my hands around his neck. "Look, Al. Back then, when I said about Luke, what I meant was..." Before he could complete, I cut him off and replied, "Liam please. Let's just be civil for tonight. At Least for our parents."

"Alright." He sighed and continued, "So, who are you going to the ball with?"

"Luke." I replied and his face turned pale. My phone rang and it saved me from another argument. I pulled myself away from Liam and took out my mobile. It was Adrian.

Right on time.

He had called to invite me to Poppy's surprise birthday party. I gladly agreed and then disconnected. Before Liam could bring back the topic, I said, "Can we go down and have dinner? I am starving."

He nodded with a faint smile and led me downstairs to the dining room.

It was almost eleven by the time we got back home. After our small conversation at the library, I made no more attempts to talk to him again at all that night. When I came back to my bedroom, I checked my phone for messages. Only one text from Adrian, 'My place tomorrow. Poppy's surprise birthday party at ten.'

My life was turning upside down and my friends were planning to surprise Poppy with a party. I was surprised enough without one. Thank you.

I woke up the next day wondering about last night and whatever happened back at Liam's. I felt a strong attraction towards Liam, but I didn't want to end up with a playboy, so I shook it off. My phone rang. It was Lucy.

"Hey Al, where are you?" She asked over the receiver.

"At home."

"Well Adrian's busy and I still need to buy a few things to buy for Ally's birthday. So I was wondering if you can come with me?"

"Why not? I will pick you up in half an hour." I said and she agreed. After ending the call, I got up from my bed and after freshening up, went downstairs.

My mom was sitting on her bed, working on her laptop. "Mom, I am going to a surprise birthday party tonight. It's organised in one of my friend's summer houses. Can I spend the night there?" I asked her. "Well yes. But call me when you reach alright?" She replied, not looking away from the screen.

Busy. Busy. Busy.

"Thanks mom." I said and made my way out.

Soon I was on my way to Lucy's house. Adrian had it all planned out for the surprise party. We were to take Poppy from Adrian's house to the summer house for the surprise. Then we would board Adrian's yacht and when the clock strikes twelve, we cut the cake. And of course Adrian had some bonus fireworks to add up to the celebration.

"Hi Ally! Right on time!" Lucy said as she got in my car. "Though there are slight changes in the plan."

"And which are?"

"Well, I will be picking up Poppy's gift from the boutique and then I will hit home for some work. You, on the other hand, will go and get the cake from the bakery for tonight's party. And don't worry, Luke will help you with it." She said as she adjusted her seatbelt. "Fine." I replied and kept driving.

After a while we reached the boutique and parked my car a few blocks away. "Why would you get Poppy a dress for her birthday? It's so common." I was all confused. "It's not an ordinary dress. It's custom made. You will know when you see it." She explained. And then a sales associate brought a box outside and walked over to us. "Check it out Al." Lucy said as she held the dress in front of me. I was shocked and wondered at the same time. The dress was magnificent. It was a lime green coloured dress, with off shoulder sleeves and really attractive lace work done halfway across the bottom. When I looked closely, I noticed that there were seashells, coffee beans, and mini Eiffel towers weaved over the lace work. There was a crystal belt around the waist as if adding up a last touch to the beauty of the dress. "What do you think? Will she like it?" Lucy asked. "Like it? Lucy, she will love it!" I exclaimed with joy.

Later after making payments, we visited a coffee shop and decided to talk over a cup of coffee. "How will you guys bring Poppy without making her guess about the party?" I asked curiously. "She has no idea. Trust me. Every year, we celebrate on her birthday eve. But this time we are doing this a day early as you see. We told her that we will be celebrating Adrian's victory he scored two days back. So I don't think she has a clue unless somebody has already slipped it out in front of her." Lucy chuckled as she finished explaining. We decided to leave after a few minutes and headed back home.

Luke called later at noon to say that he will be picking me up at six as we needed to help with the decorations. "Also if Poppy calls you, just tell her you have the flu and can't come to the party today. We will surprise her at the party." He added.

"And why can't I say I have to attend a family meeting rather than saying I have the flu?"

"Because I might have told her that you have the flu and I will be visiting my grandma's house." He giggled. "Yeah. Well done. Next time make sure to say that I was run over by a car." I replied with a pinch of sarcasm and that made us both smile.

The sun was about to set and I was still wondering about what to wear for the party. And then I finally pulled myself a turquoise-coloured strapless dress with pearls embedded in its bodice. I chose a cream-coloured heel as well. And then I took another pair of clothes and stuffed it all in a bag.

After a few minutes, Luke came to pick me up. Once I bid goodbye to mom, I walked down the driveway to Luke's car and then we drove away.

The bakery was half a mile from my house. Luke handed a coupon at the reception when we reached and after a while two men brought a huge cake outside. It was a two-tiered cake, and the moment I saw it, I started doubting if I could take it to the destination in one piece. "Please drive carefully Luke." I pleaded to him as he got in the driver seat and I sat behind with the cake.

"Don't worry Al. We will be there in no time." He tried to lighten the pressure. "No. You take your time. Poppy would love to cut it while it's still in one piece." I said nervously.

After driving for forty-five minutes, we finally arrived at the venue. The cake was saved and I finally took a sigh of relief. "Come on. I will take you to your room before we get started." Luke said and started walking upstairs. I followed him upstairs and into my room. "Well, this is it. And if you need anything, you can tell me. My room is right across the corridor." He informed me. "Well thank you." I said, grinning. He nodded and left me alone.

Once I freshened up, I went down to Luke to help with the arrangements. I walked down the front door and into the garden where all the arrangements were to be made. It was gleaming with yellow fairy lights, and antique lamps were placed around the lawn, appearing as if the garden gnomes guarded them. Helium balloons floated above the center wooden table where stood a spectacular champagne tower, and glittered cardboard cuttings were loosely tied to the strings that read the name 'Poppy'. I looked around for Luke until I finally spotted him holding on to a wooden ladder that was leaned against a red oak. He climbed down slowly and turned to me, "Hey Al. Can you climb up and put these wooden ornaments along that thin string while I go and get some more of these.

"Why not Luke?" I took the ornaments from his hand and started climbing the tree. "Maybe you should climb without your heels." He advised me but I was already halfway up. "That's alright. It's not that far up." I replied as I wrapped my thigh against the ladder and rested my arm on the tree, to start tying up the things. "Well you be careful up there." He said and walked away in search of more ornaments.

I was done with the tying by the time Luke returned. "Okay. Now you get down and let me finish it." Luke called out to me and I started descending slowly. I was halfway down when my heel slipped over a rung and I lost my balance. If my heels had any straps, I would have faced something worse but didn't. I scratched my knee over another rung, and then fell down straight to the ground on my back with a thud. The pain shot up my spine and I let out a scream in pain. Luke threw away the ornaments and came running to me. "Al, are you okay? I told you to climb without the heels!" He seemed really worried. "Somebody call a doctor already." He turned to others helplessly. I could feel a stinging sensation running up and down my back, and my head kept on getting lighter until I got all dizzy. Luke picked me up by his arms and took me to my room. I looked around and saw the staff follow him with tensed faces.

Damn I did some serious stunt up there.

"It's nothing serious Mr. Mellin. I have given her a few painkillers that will help her rest and also applied some gel on her knee. But it would be best if you can get an x-ray done by tomorrow." The doctor said as he checked my pupils and got up to leave. It had been quite a while since he started examining, and everybody was relieved finally to know that I will live.

Just kidding. It was not that serious.

Luke went out with the doctor and I lied flat on the bed for a while, staring at the white ceiling. Something was really uncomfortable, and I wanted to get rid of that feeling.

Oh I know what it is. I need to use the washroom.

I started getting up but then Luke came back and held me by my shoulder. "Al are you okay?"

"Yeah. I just need to use the washroom."

"Okay, let me help you up." He wrapped my hand around his shoulder and slowly helped me up on my feet. I felt numb, perhaps because of the painkillers, so I held onto him. "Don't lock the doors alright? I will be waiting outside." he instructed me and closed the door behind me.

It was already quarter to ten, and in fifteen minutes the others were supposed to arrive. "You go down and celebrate with them Luke. Don't wait for me." I said as he helped me back on the bed. "And leave you like this? No way." He denied with a smile. "I am fine. Just a bit drowsy because of those meds. Please go, otherwise I will feel very guilty about it." I replied with concern. "I will. But for now, I want you to close your eyes." He said and shut my eyes with his palm. I tried to open them back but couldn't. It felt like he pushed me into deep sleep. And then I heard a voice that I was longing to hear for a long time.

"Alina, darling be careful or you might fall." It was dad. He was chasing me through a meadow. I looked ahead and realised I was chasing fireflies. "I won't fall dad. I am going to fly with this..." And I tripped over a fence, bumping my head straight on the ground. Dad gasped in shock and came running at me. " Alina! Sweetie I told you to slow." He sat down and placed my head on his lap. "It hurts a lot daddy!" I cried out loud and he tried consoling me. "You are daddy's strong girl baby. Don't forget that. Now let me get you to the hospital." He took out his phone and called for an ambulance. I shook my head in fear, "No dad. Not the hospital! They will sting me with needles!" Dad laughed at my innocence and replied, "They do that to make you feel better sweetie. And when you get better, daddy will get you a teddy!" I looked in his eyes. "I want a teddy." He nodded with a smile, "Well you will get one." And then I cried out louder in pain.

But the pain was no more physical. I started crying out loud as I realised it was all a dream and that I will never see my dad again, standing at the doorstep with a teddy bear in his hand. And then as I started getting up, I felt a pair of arms wrap around me. "Alina, you are fine! You are fine Alina! it's just a bad dream." It was Lucy. She hugged me tight, until I gained my senses and let myself loosen up. Adrian, and Poppy stood by the bed, looking at me with worried eyes. "Why aren't you guys celebrating downstairs?" I asked which came out as a dry whisper. "There's no party without you Al." Poppy gave me a faint smile. "It's not like I am in a coma." I sighed. "That wouldn't have helped either." Adrian chuckled.

"Don't worry, Al. We are right here. You take rest." Lucy said. "No!" I exclaimed with annoyance. "I can't ruin your fun just like this! It's Poppy's special day guys!" Adrian nodded and said, "Well you are right. But if we have to celebrate anyways, we celebrate with you." I looked at him, wondering what he was planning afterall.

12

Okay, I am in. But I still can't walk. It hurts a lot." I explained. " Luke nodded confidently, "Yeah okay. You will be just fine. Get changed and I will take care of the rest." I wanted a more elaborate answer but he already left the room along with Adrian. Lucy closed the door and Poppy turned to me, "Okay Al. Let's get you dressed now, shall we?" She picked me up and then both of them helped me put on my party wear.

"Okay Luke. We are done here." Lucy said as she finished combing my hair. Luke opened the door and came over to me, "Good. Now let's take you downstairs." Lucy looked at me and said, "We will see you in the car, Al." Both the girls left the room while Luke started to help me up. He gently placed one hand on my waist and with the other he gently pulled me up on my feet. Pain shot over my body again and I leaned on him for support. "Damn it hurts." He slowly started lifting me off the ground. "Luke, that's okay. I can walk." I said but he didn't listen. "Well save it for later. You shouldn't strain yourself in this condition." He walked downstairs with me in his arms. I wrapped my hands around his shoulder and smiled at him, expressing my comfort.

We walked out and the driver helped us in the car. I somehow managed to get in without hitting my head on the roof while Luke got in from the other side.

We reached the docks after a couple of minutes, and then Luke scooped me up from my seat. He walked to the pier at the end of which stood Adrian's majestic yacht. The other guys were already onboard. They helped Luke get me down on a comfortable seat.

"Okay guys, now that we are all here finally, let's make the most out of this night." Adrian said and everybody else started hooting. The yacht left the shore behind and we sailed under the starry night. The cool sea breeze made us all more excited for the party. "Well it's time to cut the cake." Adrian announced as he glanced at his watch. "Well I couldn't' agree more." I said. A staff brought the cake out in the open, properly laid out and lit with candles. We circled around, waiting for Poppy to cut the cake. She walked to the cake and cut it as we sang the birthday song on top of our lungs. The crashing waves against the yacht kept us constantly balancing ourselves. Poppy took out the first slice and gave Adrian a bite off it. "happy birthday baby." He wished her and put some cream on the tip of her nose. She kissed his lips as tears of joy rolled down her cheek. We clapped and hooted for the overjoyed couple and then took our turns on taking bites off the cake.

Lucy took out her gift, leaving Poppy wide eyed with admiration. Adrian had got her a diamond bracelet and Luke a set of diamond earrings. I took out my gift and walked to her. It was a gold-plated pendant with a diamond dew drop in the middle of it. "What's all with the diamonds guys? Did I ever mention I love diamonds." Poppy said laughing politely. Adrian chuckled and said, "Well you never mentioned otherwise." Poppy hugged us all gracefully.

Ouch.

"Thank you all for the beautiful night guys." Poppy chimed with joy. "Well it's not over yet." Adrian said and placed his arms on her shoulders. "What now?" Poppy asked, all confused. "Well why don't you tell us?" He replied and pointed to the sky as he turned her gently. As soon as the clock struck twelve in the midnight, a pinkish red light flashed and then multiple rocket crackers shot up in the sky making the starry night more vibrant. It was the fireworks that Adrian had planned. The rockets went high in the sky and then burst into colourful flames, and as the sparks cleared out, we all looked at it joyously as it formed cursive letters that read, 'Happy Birthday Poppy' high up there. We all hugged Poppy from behind and wished her all the love and happiness in the world, and of course, a splendid birthday.

We got back to the shore after some time and headed back to the summer house in our cars. I didn't realize when I fell asleep in the car, but when I woke up, I realised I had been resting my head on Luke's shoulder. "Sorry, i didn't realise." I said, quickly moving away from him. "Well, you had a good nap." Luke replied and got out to help me up to my room.

As he walked upstairs with me in his arms, I said, "I know I am asking more out of this, but can you please take me to the balcony. I want to sit and watch the stars for a while." He nodded with a smile and walked to the other end of the corridor where the balcony was. He placed me down on the terrace and sat beside me.

We sat there in silence for a long time. "You can go and rest Luke. I will manage." I said finally. He turned towards me, his face just inches apart from mine. I could feel his warm breath on my face and as I looked deep in his eyes, he glanced at my lips and said, "Did anybody ever tell you that the moon makes you appear more beautiful?" I looked at his moonlit face for a second and before I knew, he crashed his lips onto mine and we kissed. At first I was not sure if I should back away, but then I realised I didn't want to. He placed his hand on my waist and pulled me closer. I didn't feel the way I felt when Liam grabbed my waist, but I did feel comfortable, for I knew that Luke would never break a heart.

And damn my naivety, I knew nothing.

13

Good morning, Al." Luke wished me as he entered my room with breakfast. The sun had risen hours ago, and I couldn't open my eyes until Luke knocked on my door and entered. The painkiller had induced a very powerful sleep last night. I could still feel my eyes closing, and if left alone I would have slept for hours again.

"Hey Luke. Good morning. Just give me five minutes, will you?" I said and headed for the bathroom.

Luke had set up the coffee table and when he saw me getting out of the bathroom, he walked over to me and placed a gentle kiss on my cheek. "How is the pain now?" He asked. "I think I am fine." I replied and sat down for breakfast. He served me eggs and said, "Well I guess you like it with the sunny side up." I chuckled and said, "Yes of course." And then he placed some bacon on my plate as I tasted the egg. "So, do I cook well?" He asked me. "One can say so." I replied with a grin. "That can be counted as a compliment." He laughed.

We could Adrian and others coming upstairs, giggling about something. They entered and looked at the two of us. "Hey love birds." Adrian chimed in while Lucy and Poppy kept giggling. I exchanged looks with Luke. "You already told them?" I rolled my eyes. "Well no he didn't have to." Lucy said as she sat beside me. "We kind of figured it out. He was blushing a lot and even cooked breakfast which was enough for us to guess."

"I am glad you guys are together. I don't know about the others, but I did see a spark between you two." Poppy said and others nodded in agreement.

Spark? Wasn't that Liam? But admitting that can break a few hearts on the breakfast table.

"Already in wonderland Alice?" Poppy said sarcastically, snapping me out of my thoughts. I blushed and said nothing. Luke placed his hands on my shoulder and looked me in the eyes, "Don't have to hide it anymore, eh?" I nodded with a smile and then noticed Lucy had walked out. "Where did she go?" I asked but before anyone could say something, she returned with a bunch of flowers. "You know, first I got you some flowers for your recovery but when I heard about last night, I had to go back and get more flowers for the couple." She laughed and said as she handed me over all the flowers. "Thank you so much Lucy." I said and delivered a smile.

"Well if you are feeling good, can we go out somewhere today?" Luke asked.

"Yeah sure. But where?" I wondered out loud.

"That will be a surprise. Now get changed." Luke said and they started walking out. "Al, do you need a hand?" Lucy offered me help but I declined politely. "I think I can manage Lucy. But thanks anyways." I said and closed the door behind them. The painkillers made my back feel numb, though the scratches on my knee stung a little.

I was not sure if I could handle myself on the stairs so I called Luke for help once I was ready to leave. He lifted me up and brought me downstairs, and now that we were sort of a couple, it felt romantic.

It didn't feel romantic last night with all that pain in my ass though.

We took off in a couple of minutes and when we were on the road, my phone rang. It was Liam and I was unsure if I should answer that, but I picked up anyway. "Hey Liam, what's up?" I said and Luke exchanged a quick look with me. "Hi Al. I was just asking that if we are cool now, can we just maybe go for lunch?" He asked over the receiver. "Well not today. I am with Adrian and others in his summer house." I replied.

"We can go tomorrow if you want."

"Yeah sure. Why not." I replied and said goodbye before I finally disconnected.

Luke had taken us all to a beach. I got down and looked at the far stretched sea. "So is this your surprise?" I said giggling. "Well no. For that we have to go a little further." The others walked to the beach and I got back in the car with Luke. He covered my eyes with an eye mask and asked me to keep it on until he removes it himself.

We got down from the car and then he held me by my shoulder and we walked for a couple of minutes. "Now, this is your surprise." Luke said as he removed the eye mask and revealed the suspense.

I was standing in front of a huge seaplane. Luke had planned this surprise so perfectly. "Luke, are we seriously going to fly on it?" I asked him. "Yes. And I am going to fly it." He replied. I was taken aback. "What? No please. Tell me you are joking." He laughed and replied, "Well I am not, and don't worry, I have an experience of over two years so I think we will be fine."

We got in the plane, and in a few minutes we were flying high in the air. I looked out of the window and saw the sea below us, shining brightly under the morning sun. "It's beautiful." I almost whispered. Luke lowered the plane above the sea slowly, and then as we surfed over the water, a few dolphins joined in and swam along with us. I clicked some pictures with Luke and catched some really good scenery as well. We landed on the water soon after that and returned back to the car.

That was some really good experience. Maybe I should try skydiving next. Well, not with this stinging pain in my back though.

Later that noon we stopped by at a restaurant near my locality, and we ordered some food. Luke casually put his arm around my shoulder. Then slowly we pulled in closer and kissed in peace. But as I drew back a while later, I looked behind him to see Liam standing across the restaurant and staring at us. I got up to say something, but he ran before that. "Liam no! Wait!" O called out to him but he was long gone. I stood there frozen near my seat.

Why do I feel guilty about it?

"Alina, come sit. Our order has arrived." Luke said as a waiter served us a few dishes. "Can we go home Luke? I don't feel like eating anymore." I said and walked away. He followed me without uttering another word.

Liam's POV

When I saw Alina kissing Luke, I didn't know what to do. I was shocked to my core. It felt as if something deep inside me broke and fell apart and would never be fixed again. I could hear her call me out but I couldn't stop. Not after what I witnessed just a few seconds ago.

I ran back to my car and drove in rage for hours. I couldn't erase the picture of her kissing Luke from my mind. She didn't know who Luke was. I decided that I will save her, no matter what. "Even if she hates me forever after it, i will still stand in front of her and tell her everything that's wrong with her and the relationship she is in." I wondered out aloud.

Alina's POV

I had called Liam several times but he just wouldn't pick up. I was a little scared because after a couple of tries , the caller feedback responded that his phone was switched off. I knew how Liam felt about me and when he saw me kiss Luke in front of him, he was definitely torn apart. "Hey Al." Adrian peeked into my room. "The weather forecast says it's going to rain heavily today. So I was thinking if maybe we could return tomorrow."

I nodded and said, "Yeah sure. I will call my mom and let her know."

"Okay cool. And the dinner will be served at seven. So be there alright?" He said and I nodded again.

Don't feel like speaking to anyone.

I had told Luke that I was having a headache, and he had come by to check on me a few times. But I wanted to be left alone. I called mom and informed her about everything. She agreed with my decision and allowed me to stay in the summer house one more night. Once I was done talking to her , I tried calling Liam again, and this time, to my surprise, he picked up. "Liam. Look, earlier what happened, I..." But he interrupted me and said, "Oh come on Alina. I am really annoyed about earlier. You consider me a friend and didn't even care to tell me about it?" I was shocked at his response.

But isn't he the one who wanted me to stay away from Luke?

"Look Al." He continued, "I am really happy for you. It's good to know that you finally have found somebody for yourself. now, let's meet up tomorrow at lunch and then we can talk eh?" And before I could say anything he said goodbye and disconnected. I sat on my bed, trying to figure out what had just happened.

Liam's POV

I didn't want her to speak and so I cut her before she could give any explanation, because that would have just hurt me more. I wanted to yell at her and tell her that Luke was not someone she can be with in a healthy relationship. But I knew if I told it to her, she would just assume that I am trying to separate her from Luke and hate me even more. So I decided to do it the hard way and when Alina realises who he is, I will be there to love her.

Alina's POV

I was swimming so deep in my thoughts that I didn't realise when it was time for dinner. Luke entered my room and hugged me from behind. "So, how does my baby feel now?" He asked as he planted kisses on my neck. "I am fine Luke, thank you." I said and turned to him. We started kissing and then all of a sudden I realised he was lifting my top slowly. "Wait Luke! What are you doing?" I shoved him away from me. "Al, come on. Just once..." He tried closing in again but I shoved him harder this time. "No Luke. I don't want to." He could feel I was getting furious. "Okay I am sorry. It won't happen again." He apologized and I just nodded. "Can we go to dinner?" He asked after a moment of silence. "Yes sure." I replied and walked downstairs with him.

The next day, after breakfast we headed back to home. Luke dropped me at my house and drove away. I came into my room, laid on the bed, and stared at the ceiling for a long time.

Let's wait for lunch now. Shall we?

14

I woke up when my alarm rang at eleven. Somehow I had slept staring at the ceiling. I took a shower, and after putting on a pair of blue jeans and a pink tank top, I walked downstairs. I could hear voices coming from the living room, and when I got down, to my surprise, Liam was already there. He was talking to my mom. "When did you come?" I asked him as I approached them. "Just a few minutes ago." He replied and then turned again to my mom, "It was really nice to talk to you Mrs. Campbell." My mom smiled at him and replied, "Come more often Liam. Have a good day." And then he walked out. "Bye mom. I will come back soon." I kissed her forehead and walked to Liam's car.

"So, where do you want to go?" He asked a while after we took off. "Wherever you want to." I replied with a smile. "Well if that's what you want, we can go for seafood." He suggested and I accepted without any questions because I was least worried about the food.

We got to a nearby barbecue special and ordered prawns and pomfret fries. Liam adjusted himself comfortably and then spoke, "So, how long?"

"Huh?" I asked in confusion.

"How long since you and Liam have been dating?" He elaborated.

"Poppy's birthday, I would say."

"Well, I am happy you finally found someone you can trust." He said sarcastically and I sensed it well enough. "It's not like that Liam. I liked him for a long time." I said, clarifying his doubts. "It's okay. I am happy for you Al." He said and then smiled. I looked at him in silence and then asked, "So tell me. Are you going with him to ski?"

What is he even talking about?

"What are you even talking about?" I asked. "The skiing, Al. Every year after the winter ball, most couples from our school go skiing." He explained. "Well, I don't know if I can…" Before I could finish, he interrupted, "Oh come on. Why won't you come. All of us will be there. And you should go anyway, since now you got yourself a girlfriend."

"So you will be there as well?."

"Well yeah, my parents have a property there." He said. "And whom are you planning to go with?" I asked curiously. "My girlfriend."

But he didn't have one.

"I thought you didn't have any." I replied with doubtful expressions. "Well now I do." He smirked and continued, "We met a while ago at the coffee shop. She was an old friend and after a few cups of cappuccinos, she confessed her love to me."

I didn't know if I was happy for him, but I was annoyed for sure. I didn't know he could change so fast. But, before I could ask anything further, our food arrived and we ate in silence for a long time. Then he finally broke the silence, "So, tomorrow is the last date for submission of the assignment. I wanted to meet you regarding that mainly." I gulped and replied, "Yes I know. I have almost completed it. What about you?"

"I have finished it already. It's in my car." He answered, looking elsewhere. "And did you finish your writing on 'love'?"

I asked. He shrugged and replied, "Yeah, you can say so. I even made a few notes so that you can compare my write-up with you." I nodded and he continued, "Or maybe you don't need to compare. you already know enough about love, don't you Al?" I choked on my food for a moment. I had to cough and then clear my throat to reply, "Everybody's not as experienced as you, Liam. I need time to understand what love really is."

"Well I hope you realize it soon, Al. And when you do, you will see it's beautiful." He replied, looking straight in my eyes.

"Yeah right." I smiled and resumed eating my lunch.

Liam's POV

Well, I don't have a girlfriend. And when asked by Alina, I definitely lied. I had seen this moment coming and already talked to a childhood friend into this. She was ready to act as my girlfriend when the time would come.

"And did you finish your writing on 'love'?" She asked me, most probably because earlier I told her that I don't believe in it and that I will have a hard time writing about it. Well, at least now I know that I believe in it.

"Well I hope you realize it soon, Al. And when you do, you will see it's beautiful." I told her finally, after taunting her about love, and watched her eating peacefully. That day was not far enough before she really gets to see how beautiful love really is.

After handing her my assignment, I dropped her home later that evening, and with a heaved heart, returned to mine. All I needed to do now was wait.

Alina's POV

I ran upstairs as soon as I got back home. I wanted to complete my assignment, and on top of that, I wanted to see what Liam had written on his part of the assignment. I quickly flipped open his file and began going through the words he had scribbled.

Love

There are different kinds of love that a human feels. It can be the love you feel for your parents, or for your siblings, or for your soulmate, but at the end of the day, it all comes down to one simple conclusion - Understanding. When you fall in love, you don't fall for his or her beauty, rather, you fall for the fact that he or she has changed your life. You fall in love because you realize that one person has changed your way of thinking, the way you look at the world, and on top of everything, that person has changed you. He or she had filled all your gaps and accepted all your angels and demons and embraced you for what you truly are.

So no matter what, you understand what love is when you decide within yourself, that no matter what, you will always protect them against all odds. Even if it has all come to one conclusion, that is separation, you will still be there for them whenever they need you and love them when they want you to. No matter how silly they are, you will hold them close to you, even when they are far away. So for me, love is nothing but a mutual understanding with a vow made to oneself, that even destiny can't change the fact that I will keep embracing love, even when it demands nothing but patience to hold on to forever, and a dream to come true.

I was unsure of how to express my feelings after reading his words. I couldn't believe that a selfish person like Liam, could hold so much in his heart. As I was about to read the second paper, the doorbell rang.

Luke stood at the door with a bouquet of roses which he sweetly handed over to me with a smile. "Missed me?" He asked me and planted a kiss on my cheek. "Thank you Li… Luke, I mean. And yes baby, I did miss you." I stammered. "Can I come in?" He asked and I politely welcomed him in.

God. Why am I thinking about Liam? Focus Alina!

We sat down in the living room and he said, "So Al, you see, every year after Winter Ball all of my friends go skiing on the mountains. So I was wondering, maybe you can join us this time."

Oh this is what Liam mentioned earlier.

"Well yeah, why not? It will be fun. So when are we leaving?" I asked him.

"A week after the ball, that is, three weeks from now."

"Oh okay! Thank God! I have so much time to pack." I chuckled and he smiled faintly.

"But, we could have talked about this on the phone. That's not all you are here for. Are you?" I smiled and smacked him playfully on his arm.

"You are right, Al. There's something else I need to talk about." He confessed and continued, "Look, I may sound jealous or possessive, but yesterday when Liam saw us kissing, I felt you really didn't like that. Now what is it? Are you guys friends again?"

My smile died instantly. I didn't know what to answer, but then I rekindled my emotions and said, "It's nothing like that Luke. After the dinner at his place, we are sort of friends now, and I didn't like him seeing us back then, because his mom is a friend of mine and I don't want anybody else to tell her about you before me. And why do you care anyways Luke? I am all yours now." That consoled him somewhat and I could tell it by the change of expressions on his face. "It's nothing, Al. I Just don't think you are happy with me." He said and I smiled at him. "I am happy with you big guy. Now let's just go somewhere and blow out this tension we have created." I said and he nodded with a smile. "Where do you want to go?" He asked. "Maybe the movies." I replied and he agreed.

After the movie, he dropped me back at my house. Mom's car was parked at the driveway and I knew she was home. So I bid him goodbye at the driveway itself with a kiss and came up to my room.

I really hope the winter brings some peace.

15

I was late for school. I put on the first thing I found to wear and headed downstairs. It was too late for breakfast, so I had to start my day with an apple. I heard my mom wish me a good day from the kitchen as I hurried to my car and took off.

I somehow made it to school on time. The first bell had rung already, so I made my way to the homeroom. After that I had English, so I walked to my locker and started taking out my books. Lucy came by as soon as she saw me in the corridor and tapped on my shoulder. "Hey Lucy." I glanced at her once and started searching through my books in the locker for my English textbook. "Hey Al. How is your back?" She asked curiously. "I am better. Thanks.' I replied.

"So, are you coming for skiing after the ball?" She asked enthusiastically. "I don't know. I will think about it." And I ruined it for her. She stood there with an annoyed face. I laughed and continued, "Just kidding, Lucy! Of course I am coming." I chimed making her enthusiasm return out of thin air. "We will have so much fun Al!" She almost squealed with excitement and that's when the bell rang. "See you later, Lucy." I said and walked to my English class. I took my regular seat at the back bench and a few seconds later, Liam came by and sat beside me.

"Are you done with the assignment?" He asked me. "Yeah, and here are your notes. It was helpful, thanks." I said and returned his file. "Not a problem. I just hope now that you know the true meaning of love?" he said and gave me a smile.

Now I wonder if his assignment was nothing but a love letter for me.

The teacher came in soon and announced, "As you all know that today is the last day for the submission of your assignments, please put it on my desk after the class." And with that, she began teaching the class.

I sat quietly, listening to her lecture, when suddenly Liam slid in a note under my notebook.

'Do you want to hang out after school?" The note read that.

"Where?" I whispered back to him?

He slid in another note - 'My place. I will pick you up at four'.

"okay done." The bell ring followed my whisper. I quickly arranged my books, submitted my assignment at the desk and left the class.

"Can I drive your car once more?" I asked him with a smile. "Never again." He chuckled nervously and I laughed.

At lunch Adrian challenged me at skiing. "Trust me Adrian, you will regret it." I said and he replied ecstatically with confidence, "Make me." I nodded with a scoff and he drew his hand out as if throwing a challenge at me. "Let's do this." I said and shook his hands.

Later while I was busy digging in my food, my phone chimed. It was Luke.

Do you want to hang out after school with me?

I could not put down Liam's invitation as it will ruin things more between us and I didn't want to lie to him either.

Sorry honey. I am going to Liam's place.

Luke saw my text but did not reply back. I knew I had pissed him out but it was better to tell the truth than lie to him.

Or was it?

Liam's POV

I never thought Alina would agree to hangout with me after school. I thought she might have some plans with Luke and thus, would deny mine. But since she had finally agreed to it, I was happy to be around her as a friend. I went to a nearby shop and bought flowers for her. I picked up roses, daisies and sunflowers, making sure that I don't leave anything behind that she would love to see.

I had my butler, James, to prepare something special for dinner and to place all of the fresh flowers in vases and organise it all in a presentable manner. Finally, I took a shower, wore a purple buttoned-down shirt along with a pair of blue jeans and walked out of my house. She had always admired Lamborghinis, so I took out the one in emerald blue, and headed for her house.

Alina's POV

I took a quick shower, and changed into an orange floral dress. As I was putting on my heels, my phone rang. It was Liam.

"Hey Al. I am waiting downstairs."

"Just give me five minutes and I will be down there."

"Okay. And pick up a swimming suit with yourself, would you?"

"Alright." I said and disconnected the call.

It's a good time for a swim.

After doing the needful, and locking my house, I walked out just to see a beautiful Lamborghini parked in my driveway with Liam standing right next to it. "I have to admit, you have quite a collection of cars, Liam." I said as I admired the beauty in blue. "Well, what can I say? A man has his hobby." He said as he entered the car.

We settled inside and buckled up. Liam delivered an appealing smile and said, "I thought you would deny to hangout with me anymore." I turned to him and stared at him in silence for a moment, and then I said, "Well I had to give it a try." But deep inside I knew that there was more. Liam couldn't read my face and witness the agony beneath it, but little did he know that I was not going to let him walk away after what he did to Lucy. That night when Luke and I had our first kiss, Lucy reminded me of the pain he had given her.

Flashback

"Did anybody ever tell you that the moon makes you appear more beautiful?" Luke said and then before I knew it we were deeply involved in kissing. But then I heard the balcony door squeak, and when I looked up, I saw Lucy standing right on the other side of the door. Her eyes were red, and tears rolled down her cheeks. As soon as she realized that I had seen her, she wiped away her tears and walked away from there.

After saying good night to Luke, I went to Lucy's room and knocked on her door. "Come on in." She said in a cheerless voice. "Lucy what's wrong?" I asked her. "I didn't feel like ruining your moment Al." She said, wiping away her tears. "Well you wouldn't have anyways Lucy. Now, if you consider me a good friend, tell me what made you cry?" I said placing a hand on her shoulder. She took a deep breath and said, "Seeing you kiss, I was reminded of me and Liam. He would kiss me the same way and tell me all those beautiful things that I always dreamt to hear from someone, Al. I knew how he was, and I was nothing like the other girls he dated. He always used to tell me that we were temporary, and I kept on trying to love her immensely like a fool. I gave my heart to him, and he broke it Al. I try to mend it everyday, but I think the scars he has given me, will never let me trust someone ever again." And then she started crying even more. I hugged her tightly and said nothing but let her cry.

Crying had healed me. Crying will heal her.

And that day I made a promise to myself that no matter how far I have to take this, I will give Liam the taste of his own medicine someday.

Flashback Ends

"Alright. We are here." Liam said, making me snap out of my thoughts. I smiled and looked at his mansion. "Are your parents here?" I asked. "No. They are in Paris." He said and got out of the car.

"So tell me what would you want to do?" He asked me with a glowing smile.

"Well, why don't we swim already? Isn't that why you made me pack my suit?" I suggested and he gestured to me with open hands, showing me the way to his swimming pool.

Liam's swimming pool was nothing like a regular one that one could find in almost any high earning family's backyard. It was way too classic. The backyard was decorated with exotic plants, placed along both the sides of the swimming pool. The swimming pool stretched all the way to the end of his backyard, thus making it seem like a river. On the other end, one can admire a man built rocky structure, from which an artificial waterfall rained down in the swimming pool, giving it altogether an exquisite look.

I stood there, lost in its beauty for a moment. "Well then, shall we?" Liam asked as he walked up to me. "Yes. I will go and get changed." I replied and walked to the changing room beside the pool.

I changed into a bikini and went outside. It was a beautiful sunny day, perfect for swimming. Suddenly my phone rang, and I answered it without checking the caller ID.

"Hello."

"Hi Al, where are you now?" It was Poppy.

"I...um...I am at Liam's place," I replied honestly, having no reason to lie.

"What are you doing at Liam's house? I thought you guys were no longer friends, and Luke called me to ask if you were hanging out with me. What is going on Ally?" Poppy inquired suspiciously.

"Poppy, did you tell Luke that I am not with you?" I asked, panicking.

If Luke finds out I am spending time with Liam, instead of him, he would freak out.

"I didn't give him a proper reply but seriously, what is going on?"

"Poppy, could you please tell him that I am with you. I promise I will explain everything to you later." I requested.

"Okay, but we really need to talk about this soon," she said in a serious tone.

"Of course, Poppy, I'll be grateful..."

"Don't thank me yet, we'll meet the cafe downtown after you come back from your trip to America. Bye!" She said.

"Bye, Poppy!" I said as I hung up the phone.

Phew! That was close. Poppy is a life saver. Now I need to go and carry on with my plan.

Liam's POV

I was mesmerised when I saw Al walking into the pool. She was looking so hot in that lime green bikini. She slowly walked to a nearby wooden chair, kept her things on it and dived into the pool.

"Whose idea was it to give this design to the pool?" Al asked.

"My mom's, she wanted a tropical feel while swimming," I replied.

"That was a really nice thought. It looks beautiful," she said and started swimming towards me. "I have a challenge in mind."

"And what is that?" I asked.

"The first person to swim back and forth two laps from this end to that, wins," she said pointing towards the opposite end of the pool. "And if I win, you will do whatever I say for one day."

"And if I win you will go skiing with me," I said.

"Deal," she extended her hand for a handshake.

"Deal," I said and shook her hand.

I am one of the best swimmers at school but I shouldn't really judge her. She might be better than me.

Alina's POV

"So, let's go to the start line, but first we need someone to be the referee," I told Liam.

"You are right, just give me five minutes and I will be back," Liam said as he exited the pool and picked up his phone to call someone.

After two minutes, a man in his late thirties approached the pool.

"So who is that man?" He stood a few feet away to my right.

"He is my butler, James, and he will be our referee for our challenge today," Liam said.

"Okay, let's start."

"I'll count till three. Jump when I tell you to. Is that clear?" James asked and we nodded.

The moment I heard 'jump', I dived in and started swimming. After completing my first lap, I saw Liam was ahead of me.

He must be very happy but he has no idea how good I am!

We were swimming back to the finish line after the second lap, we were neck and neck. As I reached the other end of the pool, I quickened my pace, kicked my legs harder, and....I made it! I beat the all-time swimming champion! I quickly left the water for some much-needed air.

"Miss. Alina, you won," James announced once I was out, and I grinned, and then I looked at Liam.

"How the heck did you do that?" He looked shocked.

"Well, all my time spent underwater has paid off finally," I gave him an evil smile.

"Well, then, when do you want to spend the day with me?"

"Well, I'll let you know about that later. I think it's getting dark, so we should probably go back inside, and I'm famished after all this swimming." I exited the pool and dried myself off with a towel.

" Alright, I think we should celebrate your win, so let's go back inside."

" James, could you please tell the workers to prepare the dinner, we'll be there in an hour," he asked James.

" Sure, Sir!" James replied and went away.

"Come on, I'll show you the guest room so you can shower and change," Liam said.

"Well, then, lead the way," We walked away from the pool.

It took me around forty-five minutes to shower and get ready. I went down wearing a pencil skirt and a red floral top, with my hair still wet from shower.

"Ah, finally somebody got ready. Come, let's have dinner," Liam said, pulling a chair for me.

"Thank you so much!"

"So, Al, tell me what is it about spending a day with me?" He looked curious.

"Trust me Liam, you'll have so much fun. I have everything planned." I left him wondering.

Once dinner was over we went into the living room for some coffee and chat.

"So how did she actually propose to you?"

"Oh, that. It was like..." he paused mid-sentence because my phone rang, and I answered it.

"Hi, Mom! What is it?" I asked.

"Hi, Hun! Where are you?"

"I am at a friend's place, Mom. What happened?"

"Oh okay, but don't forget we have to go to your aunt's place tomorrow and the flight is at 3 a.m," she said.

"Oh, yes! I completely forgot about that. I'll be there in ten," I said and hung up.

"So, I guess our day trip ends here," I said, turning to Liam.

"I really had a great day, Al. Come, I'll drop you home," he said and we made our way out of the house.

16

Alina, wake up, Hun!" My mother said. "We are getting late."

When I slowly opened my eyes I saw she was already dressed for the flight, I panicked and grabbed my phone from the bedside table.

"Oh, God! Did I sleep too long?" I asked, panicked. "It's 2 a.m., we have one hour to get to the airport. So sorry, Mom. I'll take just five minutes to get ready." I got up and rushed to the bathroom. I took a refreshing hot shower. When I got out, I heard my mom shouting.

"Alina, the car is here."

I quickly went to my closet, wore a top and a pleated skirt, grabbed my phone and purse, and ran downstairs.

"Lock the front door before you come," she shouted before she went inside the car. I grabbed a cereal bar, locked the door and ran outside to get in as well. It took us almost ten minutes to get to the airport, we rushed through all the checkpoints. We made it to the terminal just before the gates closed. I started to relax once we were seated inside the plane. This was my first time on a flight. Normally, my family takes a private jet everywhere we go and we never really had to rush. The jet used to be there waiting for us, but now nothing was the same, and I absolutely despised it.

"Mom," I said.

"Yes, Alina?" She asked.

"Will our lives be like this hereafter?"

"Yes honey, I am afraid so." That made me really sad.

I was jet lagged and exhausted when we arrived. At the exit, my mother's younger sister, my Aunt Sally, was waiting for us. She and my Grandmother are the only relatives I know. I don't know anybody from my dad's side.

"Oh my goodness, I'm seeing you after so long my Cupcake! How are you?" My aunt screamed as she embraced me in a bone crushing hug.

"I..um..fi..ne," I said, unable to breathe properly. Once she let go of me, I quickly filled my lungs with the much-needed air.

"Hi, Linda!" my aunt said, turning to my mom giving her a tight hug too.

"Nice seeing you again, Sally. Shall we leave?" My mom asked.

"Sure, c'mon." We headed towards Aunt's car.

When we reached home, I saw Uncle Mike waiting for us at the front door. I am always very happy to see him. He is the most fun person to have around.

"Hello, Sugar Plum! So you survived the bear hug?" Uncle Mike asked as we entered the house.

"Yes Uncle Mike, somehow I managed to. I believe I have a long life ahead of me," I sarcastically replied before hugging him.

"So how is your research going?" I inquired. Uncle Mike has such a personality that no one would believe he is a Researcher.

"Pretty good. Do you know I am planning to go skydiving later. Do you want to join me?" He asked. He always takes me along whenever he plans to do some crazy and adventurous stuff.

"Yeah, I would love... "

"No, Mike. She is not going out and jumping out of a plane with you. She is going to spend some time with her aunt. Right, Alina?" My aunt interjected. They don't have their own children and they always treat me as their own. They are very protective of me. I feel adored and loved when I'm with them. I feel like it is my home.

"So when are we going to see Grandma?" I asked while we were all drinking coffee in the kitchen.

"I think after you freshen up and get some rest," my aunt answered.

Oh, finally, I am going to see Grandma, one of the best people I know. All I wish for is her to live a long life. After that heart attack she had, I always feel scared that I might lose her.

"Hey, Al. Why don't you come and spend your holidays with us?" Uncle Mike asked.

"I'd really like to but I can't." I had a hurt look on my face.

"Why is that?" he questioned, perplexed.

"Because I'm going skiing with my friends," I told him.

"Oh, that's bad. Poor kids! They have no idea who they're going to play against."

"I know, it'll be fun," I replied.

After that, I went up to my room and took a shower. Once I changed my clothes, I checked my phone and saw a few messages from Luke. I called him back.

"Hi, Luke!"

"Hi, Darling! How was the flight?"

"It was good. We got here like half an hour back."

"And how is your grandma?" He asked.

"I don't know yet, we will be going to see her soon," I told him

We talked for about an hour and after that I fell asleep. It was five in the evening when I woke up. I got dressed and went downstairs.

"Linda, you should file a case against that bastard," I heard my aunt say.

"No, Sal. It's not worth it," my mom replied.

"If you say so, but I really feel you should," Aunt said as I entered the living room.

"Aren't we going to see Granny? We have to leave back for England tonight, right?" I asked.

"Of course, we're going, Cupcake! We were just waiting for you to get ready." After some time, all of us headed out. It was a fifteen-minute drive to the hospital.

Once we got near the room where Grandma was, I quickly pushed open the door. She was lying on a bed. She had a huge smile on her face when she saw me. I went closer to her. "Alina, I was waiting for you," she said, opening her arms for a hug.

"I missed you, Grandma," I said, hugging her.

"Oh, I missed you more dear," she replied.

"How are you doing now?" I caressed her hair.

"I am feeling much better with you here." We went on talking for long before it was time for me to leave.

"Bye, Alina! Keep visiting dear," she said.

"I will, for sure," I said, planting a kiss on her forehead."

Oh for God's sake, please stop ringing.

I was too exhausted to get up, and someone was constantly calling me. I managed to somehow pick it up.

"Hello, who is it?" I asked in a grumpy tone.

"Ally, are you still in the 1970s where there are just landlines and no mobile phones?"

I slowly got out of bed, rubbed my eyes, and checked the caller ID, it was Poppy

"I'm sorry Pop, I was exhausted from the flight. What's up?" I asked.

"In case you forgot Ally, we're going to meet at the cafe in an hour." she sounded disappointed.

*Oh sh*t, I totally forgot about that, I owe Poppy an explanation.*

"I'll be there on time Pop, don't worry," I said.

"You better be or else I'll come to your home and drag you out even if you are wearing the worst possible outfit." Poppy knows how much I hate going somewhere in an unfit dress.

"I'm coming to pick you up anyway," She said.

"You don't need to. I have my car here."

"Well, I've set a date for you. Luke is coming to the cafe at 5." Poppy and her games.

"Okay, Pop. Bye. I need to get ready."

"Bye, see you soon," she replied.

How the hell am I gonna be on time? And on top of that I've a date. Well done, Alina!

It took me about an hour to get ready. I got myself dressed in a black jeans and cream top, matched it with my favourite laced black heels and a cream-coloured clutch. I was waiting in the living room, scrolling through the messages on my phone when

I heard somebody honk. I knew it was Poppy, I got up and made my way outside the house. I got inside Poppy's car and we were off to Central London. It took us only five minutes to reach the cafe. After parking the car, we went inside, bought ourselves coffee and took a seat near the window.

"I can't wait longer. Spill it out now. What were you doing at Liam's?" Poppy asked.

I told her each and everything. From the time I saw Lucy crying to the time I decided to take revenge, I gave her all the details of everything that has happened.

"What are you exactly trying to do? Befriend him and then abandon him?" Poppy asked.

"Yes, I want him to know how it feels. If you had seen Lucy that night, you'd know how devastated she was," I replied.

"I understand how you feel, Ally, but if Lucy would have wanted revenge, don't you think Adrian and I would already have already made it difficult for Liam to live peacefully? Lucy doesn't want to dig up old graves and so I advise you to let the bygones be bygones. Don't mix the past with the present." Whatever she was saying was very convincing.

"Also another thing," she continued. "I feel I can give this piece of advice to you being your best friend. I want to ask you to please use your heart and not your brain to decide who you love, otherwise it will be a mess." I didn't quite understand what she was implying here.

"Do you think I'm with the wrong guy?" I asked.

"I leave it to you to answer that to yourself."

Before I could ask her to explain anything, Luke came.

"Hey Al, hey Poppy." He gave a kiss on my cheek.

"Hey Luke, nice seeing you. I think I will now leave you guys alone. I also have to go see Adrian," Poppy got up to leave.

"Bye, Pop!" I said and then Luke and I got into talking.

"So where are we going?" I asked him.

He told me it's a surprise and then we left the cafe. We drove for around twenty minutes before reaching our destination.

"Here we are." We were at a carnival.

"Luke, don't you think we should act our age?" I teased him.

"We are never too old for fun, Al. C'mon," he said and got down the car.

We held each other's hand, walked to the ticket counter and bought the tickets.

"Which ride do you want to go on, Al?" He asked.

"The giant roller coaster," I said, excited.

"What are you waiting for, then?" He pulled my hand to take me towards the ride.

We took our seats and waited for the ride to start. I was scared and excited at the same time. Our seat slowly went up, I'm sure I crushed Luke's hand at one point. It ascended to the top very slowly and stopped at the highest point. While descending down and going through all the curves, the ride took an insane speed and both of us screamed at the top of our lungs. It was breathtaking. Even after stepping down the ride, I couldn't let go of Luke's hand, I was that scared.

"Oh my god, that was great! Can we do that again?" I asked Luke

"We have many rides to go on, Al, and the bones in my hand already feel crushed." He laughed. I hit him hard on the arm and we laughed again.

We went on almost every ride and after a while it made us very tired. We then decided to buy ice-cream and popcorn. We found an empty bench, sat on it and started eating.

"Luke, I think you might get sick eating that ice-cream." I took the ice-cream from his hand and started eating it too.

"Al, you have already had two. I don't think it won't be me who'll get sick," he said and tried to take it back from me.

"Okay, why don't we share?" I made a puppy face and he agreed.

We went for a boat ride after that. "What lake is this again?" I asked.

"It is the all-fall-deep-in-love lake." He knew he was saying something very nonsensical.

"You know it practically doesn't make sense," I said and he smiled.

Once the ride started, it took us inside a cave-like structure. At first, it was all dark and then I saw there was a person on the edge playing a violin and then a woman who gave us champagne. It was all so romantic. After a while rose petals were showered from above.

"Did you personally ask for all of this? I have never seen all these before in a carnival?" I asked Luke.

"Maybe I did." He came very close to me.

"I like you so much, Al," he whispered and kissed me softly on the lips at first. We then got even closer and got almost lost in each other. I wrapped my hands around his neck and he around my waist, and we did not stop kissing. For a while I had no sense of where we were, all I could see was him. I never thought that my day would end so beautifully.

"I like you even more now," I said, and we kept looking into each other's eyes for a long time.

17

Good morning, Ally! I see you had a good day yesterday," Poppy greeted me when I got out of my car.

"Well kind of, yes," I said shyly.

"Oh look who is blushing!" She started teasing me.

"Shut up, Pop! I know you and Adrian have done far more than that."

"You are right, we are experts. Want some advice?" She gave a sarcastic smile.

"Well, no. Thanks. Let's head to the class before it is too late." We entered the school building.

"You are right. I am having a test today. Bye, Ally! See you later!" Poppy said and rushed to her class and I went into mine.

I had a History test that day and honestly, I hate the subject. I was sitting in the class, praying that I pass with a B grade. The other students came in and took their seats. The teacher came and handed out the test papers. I felt like stabbing myself after seeing the questions. I couldn't remember a single thing that was asked. When you give in a lot of effort to remember something, it becomes even more difficult to recall. I somehow managed to finish the paper just before the bell rang. I had another class to attend so I left for that.

By the time school got over, all my energy had drained, but at the same time I felt happy that I was done with all the tests. I just wanted to go home and relax. I went towards the parking lot and saw Poppy, Lucy and Adrian standing near Poppy's car.

"Hey, guys! So how was the day?" I asked.

"It was good. I am very excited for the Winter Ball," Poppy said.

"So Ally, there is a ritual you will have to follow before we go to the Ball," Adrian said with a smirk.

"Uh.. Is it mandatory?" I asked, scared. Adrian always comes up with something very stupid.

"Definitely, it is. Even more that you are Luke's girlfriend," Adrian said and I looked at Poppy helplessly.

"Well, I can't help you this time. I had to go through the same thing. It was Luke who started it. I suffered, now it's your turn," Poppy said and it made me even more scared.

"At least tell me what I am getting myself into."

"It is a ritual or tradition whatever you say. It will only be revealed when you get there," Adrian said. I then turned to Lucy.

"Sorry Ally, I can't tell you either but trust me it will be fun," she said.

"I'm hoping you guys will tell me something that can guide me through it."

"That we can happily do for you, don't worry! And don't forget we are getting dressed at my place. It is a part of the tradition that we are having for the past three years," Poppy said
.

"Oh I don't mind that. Is there anything I need to know at this point?" I asked.

"You better bring extra clothes," Lucy chimed. "And when you are coming to my place, please do not wear heels," Poppy added.

"And wear jeans and a top, don't wear any dress because that will not be.. um.. appropriate," Adrian said and I was about to ask why but then he explained that these are the rules and they can't be changed. "And yes you are not supposed to see Luke that whole day or talk to him on the phone."

"What is this? I am not going to get married or anything," I said, shocked.

"No, but Luke might tell you about it." Adrian was persistent.

"Fine. I won't see him or call him or text him. Happy?" I sighed.

"Yes we are very happy," Poppy and Lucy together shouted.

I then got into my car and headed home. Once I reached the driveway, I saw my mother's car already parked there but there was another black Porsche with it. I couldn't recognise whose that was. I went inside and saw my mom sitting on a sofa and Luke on a couch beside her. Luke came up to me and kissed me on my cheek. I blushed a little.

"Oh Alina, why didn't you tell me you have such a sweet boyfriend?" My mom asked

"Sorry, Mom! I was going to introduce him to you earlier but you were never home."

"Never mind. Now that I know him already it's fine. Come sit with us," she said.

"So Luke you never told me you were coming," I inquired.

"I wanted to surprise you. Anyway, I think you now know the plan for Sunday, right?" He asked and I nodded.

"So can we go out today if you are free?"

"Sure," I said and then looked at my mom for confirmation.

"Alright, Hun, but be back early." She got up from the sofa

"I have some work to do so. See you later, Luke!" She said

"Sure, Mrs. Campbell" he said, giving her a charming smile. Luke and I then went outside and he took me to a flower shop.

"So why are we here?" I asked him, entering the shop.

"well, every year before the Ball we decorate Poppy's house with everyone's favorite flowers," he said.

"You mean the entire house?" I asked, shocked. "Isn't that too much?"

"Well not the entire house but everyone's room," he replied.

"Oh, okay," I said and Luke started ordering flowers. He turned to me to ask what my favourite flower was.

"Lavender," I said, smiling. Purple makes me happy.

Once that was done we went to a bakery and bought some pastries. We sat on a bench to eat.

"So are you excited?" He asked.

"Yes, and nervous too," I confessed.

"Don't worry! I will always be there for you," he said and pulled me for a kiss. Oh, I already love him so much!

18

Alina, your phone is ringing," my mom called from the kitchen.

"I will be down in ten minutes, mom. Let the phone ring, I'll call back later," I told her.

The last day with Luke was amazing. The flowers, the pastry, that kiss on the bench, it was all beautiful. I was playing all those moments again and again in my head. I went downstairs and checked my phone. It was Liam who had called. I called him back.

"Hi, Liam! Why did you call?" I asked when he picked up the phone.

"Al, did you forget about the deal we had? I must spend an entire day with you, remember?" He asked.

"Oh, I am free today. I will come pick you up at 10," I said.

"Yeah 10 is fine but can I drive?" He asked.

"Of course not! You will be listening to me all day and this is what I want," I said.

"But Al, I.."

Before he could finish I cut the call and went to my room to get dressed. While I was getting ready, Luke messaged.

LUKE: Shall we have lunch today?

ME: I am a bit occupied. Can we go tomorrow?

LUKE: No, that's fine. I have work. Bye!

I don't know what was wrong with him. I thought I would solve that later. I applied some lip gloss, took my phone and went downstairs and out to the garage to get my car. It didn't take me long to reach Liam's house.

"Hi, hop in," I said as I parked my car in Liam's driveway.

"Hi Al, you know that of..."

"You know the rules, Liam," I said, interrupting him.

"Okay, now till I drive I will ask a few questions and you will have to answer them honestly," I said.

"Okay, that seems easy," he said.

"Have you ever fallen in love with somebody in your life?" I asked my first question.

Liam's POV

"Have you ever fallen in love with somebody in your life?" She asked me.

I knew I had no other option but to reply.

"No, not until now," I replied.

"Hmm, okay. Next question. Why did you play with girls' feelings and hurt them intentionally?" she asked. I did not know how to reply. All this while I thought Al had started trusting me but she still thought of me as a playboy.

"Because those girls are with me only because of my looks, my wealth and for who my parents are in the society. No one has ever really loved me for who I am. I knew that and I didn't want to get hurt," I answered truthfully.

I had never really felt loved either at my house, because my parents were always traveling, or in my relationships. I always felt lonely. That is the reason I shut everyone out but with Al, it was different. The first day we met, it was different from all other experiences I had with other girls. If I would have accidentally spilled coffee on any other girl I know they would have blushed and flirted, but Al, she scolded me.

"Hello! Earth to Liam!" Al said, bringing me out of my thoughts.

"Sorry, what did you ask?" I asked.

"Okay, next. Why did you even date Lucy?" She asked.

"Oh so this the problem you had all along. Why couldn't you be straight forward? I would have told you without this stupid game," I said, and I was angry. It was about her friend all this time.

"Just answer the question, Liam!" She said.

"Fine, if that's what you want. Yes, I dated Lucy, but I warned her at the start of our relationship that I will never have feelings for her and she agreed to it. It was just a friendly casual relationship. I liked her, she was funny and all. It was all going well until she started getting messages from someone who convinced her that I loved her. It was an unknown number and she thought that it was me using indirect means to confess. It all turned really bad when she attended a party at my place with her friends. I got really drunk that day and so I went out into the balcony to get some fresh air. She came there claiming that she got a message from an unknown number to get there. She asked me to confess everything. I tried telling her that it was not me but slowly with me being drunk it became difficult. Things started seeming blur and I kissed her but not for long. When I woke up the next morning I realized what I did so that is when I broke up with her. I didn't want to complicate things any further and once everything with her ended, she stopped getting texts from that unknown number. I still feel sorry for what I did to Lucy but I didn't want to talk to her anymore." I finished telling everything and turned to look at Al. She was completely blank.

"So are you sure you weren't that unknown number who led Lucy to all that chaos?" She asked in a quiet voice.

"No," I replied sadly.

"I never saw Lucy in that manner, Al. I considered her as one of my close friends. She was always bubbly and full of energy," I said.

"Then who the hell is that person who did those things?" She asked, frustrated.

"I don't know," I replied.

Alina's POV

"I don't know," he replied.

Someone else had done it all and I needed to find who it was. After that conversation, we did not speak much and drove silently. Liam's phone rang.. It was his girlfriend asking her to meet at the cafe. He asked me to drop him there and I did. I went back home still thinking about everything he told me.

19

The big day had come, and I was anxious, excited, and a little scared all at once. I had packed my bag the night before, and I was sitting at the kitchen table eating breakfast. I still can't believe what Liam told me, but I know it's real because I saw it in his eyes, but who could that unknown be? Who would want to harm Lucy? These questions had been worrying me for a long time. I was lost in these questions when my mom entered the kitchen.

"So, when are you leaving for Poppy's house?" She inquired as she poured herself a cup of black coffee.

"In half an hour," I replied.

"So, will you be returning home tonight or staying at Poppy's?" She asked.

"I believe I will be staying at Poppy's, mom," I told her.

When I arrived at Poppy's place, I parked my car in the driveway, got out, and took my bags from the boot, making my way to the front door. When I knocked, a butler replied.

"Good morning, Miss Campbell! Here let me carry your bags to your bed," he offered.

"Thank you, are my friends here yet?" I inquired after handing him my bags.

"Yes ma'am, they are waiting for you in the pool area," he answered.

"Well thank you for that," I said and made my way to the pool area, where I saw all of them sitting in the pool chairs. Adrian noticed me and waved his hand.

"Hi Ally ho...oh shit Al..." I slipped and fell, it was too late for Adrian to alert me.

"Oh no, that hurts."

"I think I told you Ally not to wear shoes," Adrian said, as Luke, Adrian, and Poppy ran up to me.

"Yeah, but I forgot," I responded, wincing in pain.

"Well, I guess the next time you would remember," Adrian chuckled.

"And what made me slip?" I asked Luke as he helped me get up and was now carrying me towards a chair.

"Well, you slipped on rose petals," Luke answered.

"How can I slip on rose petals?" I asked, perplexed.

"Easy if those rose petals were on a wet floor and you came running in wearing heels," Adrian said. I gave him an annoyed look.

"How are you feeling now, Ally? I told Adrian it was a stupid idea and not to do it but he had to," Poppy said with concern.

"Hey I wanted them to stay on the ground. It isn't my fault that Ally Tally is so sloppy," Adrian said.

"That's alright, Pop. You can't explain things to people without a brain, so leave it," I said sarcastically, and we all chuckled, with Adrian attempting but failing to show his angry face, after which we all went back inside to get ready.

I was in the shower for around two hours enjoying the bath. When I came out of the bathroom with a towel wrapped around me, I saw Poppy in my room.

"Ally, did you sleep back in there or what?" she asked.

"Huh, no."

"Okay, once you get dressed come to my room. I will do your makeup, okay?"

"Yeah, sure," I replied.

I got myself in a beautiful maroon dress and while I was struggling with the zip on the back, I heard a familiar voice.

"Can i help you with that?" It was Luke.

"Sure and why aren't you ready yet?" I asked him when he closed the door and came in.

"Well, I don't take four or five hours to get dressed," he replied with a smirk on his face.

I smiled hearing that, he came close to me and I could feel his heart racing faster. He slowly trailed his finger along my back which sent a shiver down my back. I quickly turned towards him.

"I think I will be happy if you can close my zip, thank you!" I told him with a nervous smile.

"Fine," he said, giving a smile.

"I think you better get ready, don't want you getting late," I said, pushing him out of my room.

"I am leaving only if you give me a kiss first," he said so I quickly gave him a kiss which did not last long.

"Hey, that is not fair," he said.

"You will get more later. Now go and get dressed fast."

I went to Poppy's room to get my hair and makeup done.

"Ally, do you know that your hair is the best to work with?" Poppy exclaimed while pinning a strand of my hair using a crystal pin. "Hmm and done," she said.

"Oh wow, that looks great Pop, thank you so much!" Poppy had done an amazing job.

"Now if you're done admiring yourself, shall we leave? The boys are waiting for us downstairs," Lucy said.

"Sure, let's go," I said, and all three of us went towards the staircase. Poppy and Lucy went down first, and I was the last. When I went down, Luke was staring at me like there was no tomorrow.

"Like what you see?" I mocked him.

"I can't tell you how ravishing you look! I'm so lucky to have got a beautiful girlfriend like you," he whispered in my ears.

"If you two are done looking at each other, shall we leave?" Adrian said and I slowly stepped away from Luke. Luke put his arms around my waist and we all walked outside to the Limo. Adrian assisted Poppy and Lucy in entering before entering himself, and Luke assisted me in pulling my dress inside before closing the door.

The venue where the ball was being held was more like a mansion from the nineteenth century. The walls were made up of brick stones, and huge pillars stood at the entrances. The entire building was decorated with fairy lights and red roses. To say the least, this was one of the most magnificent places that I have ever seen.

"Shall we head inside?" Luke asked me, bringing me back from my dazed state. I realised that we had already parked and that everyone had gone inside.

"Sure," I said with a smile on my face and placed my right hand on his shoulder so that he could help me in getting out. After the driver left us, Luke and I both made our way inside.

It turned out to be the best night of my life.

20

Urgh, this is why I don't drink anymore. I'm having a horrible headache.

I was rolling around, holding my head when I heard the door of my room open. I turned to see who it was. Poppy was standing there with a coffee mug in one hand and a card of aspirin in the other.

"Good morning, Ally! How is your head doing?" She asked as she approached my bed.

"Oh god, it's horrible, I shouldn't have drunk that much," I said, exhausted.

"Here, drink this coffee and take these tablets, you'll be fine," she said, handing me the coffee and the aspirin."

"Where are the others?" I asked.

"Downstairs, tending to their hangover," she replied. After rubbing my eyes and trying to get rid of the sleep, I looked at Poppy. She looked fresh as a flower.

"Hey, how come you don't have a hangover?" I asked, confused.

"Because I don't drink," she replied. "Now freshen up and come downstairs. Breakfast in twenty minutes," she said and left the room. After ten minutes of tossing and turning on the bed, I got up and took a shower, changed my clothes and went downstairs .

"Morning Ally Tally, did Mama Bear take care of your hangover?" Adrian asked, smiling, and he got a smack on the arm from Poppy for that.

"Ouch Pop Tart, that hurts," Adrian whined.

"Pop Tart, that's a cool nickname," I laughed.

"Well, Bubble Butt, you told me you would never call me that in front of everyone," Poppy sarcastically said, and Adrian turned scarlet red when he heard that.

"Pop, was it necessary to call me that in front of Ally?" He asked, now feeling very embarrassed.

"Oh, Adrian. I am never going to stop calling you with your proper name....Bubble Butt," I said sarcastically and doubled over with laughter.

"Ally, will you please stop calling me that? I won't ever call you by a nickname," he begged.

"Good morning, everyone! So what is so funny early in the morning?" Luke asked as he entered the kitchen.

"Apparently, Ally here found out what we call Adrian in private," Poppy said, happily.

"Oh so I am free to call you by your real name Bubble Butt. Good to hear that, and I had told you she was going to find out sooner or later," Luke replied as he approached me.

"Oh shut up, I'm leaving," Adrian said as he rushed out of the kitchen with Poppy following him, leaving me and Luke alone in the kitchen.

"I'm sorry for last night, Al…" he began.

"No, it's alright, I understand how you might be feeling, but Luke, I need some time," I answered.

"Al, how long are you going to take because honestly I have to tell you something. You aren't spending enough time with me and you are giving me mixed signals too, so please find out what you exactly want," he said, frustrated.

"I...I am so sorry Luke. I know but I promise that I do like you," I said slowly as I stood up and kissed him. At first he didn't react but then he gave in and kissed me. The kiss slowly got intense but then we were interrupted by somebody coughing and we quickly broke off.

"Sorry guys, no PDA in the kitchen, please," Lucy said as she took an apple and sat down. I blushed profusely.

"Sorry Lucy, we didn't see you," I said.

"Nah, never mind," she said.

"I got to pack, see you guys later," I said as I kissed Luke goodbye.

I quickly started packing when I got to my room because the sooner I would be able to get home, the sooner I could finish packing for our trip. While I was packing, Poppy entered my room.

"Hey," I said.

"Can we talk?" She asked.

"Sure Pop, what is it?" I inquired.

"Are you and Luke doing fine? I'm sorry Ally, but I couldn't stop myself from hearing you two talk."

"I don't know Poppy, I know that Luke's a good guy but I don't know why I can't go beyond kissing when it comes to being physical with him," I told her honestly.

"Al, I think you should sort out your feelings about Luke and Liam," Poppy said, and I was taken aback.

"Pop, Liam and I are just friends. He is a playboy. I consider him only a friend," I said.

"Well, I believe you, but remember that whatever decision you make, I will always support you," she said. This was something that my dad used to tell me and nobody else has ever said this to me after him. I felt my eyes prick with tears. I then walked over to her and hugged her.

After reaching home, I went straight to my room and into my bed to sleep. No other place can ever give you that comfort.

"Oh, is that your boyfriend sweetie?" my father mocked as Jacob walked out the door.

"No dad, that's my project partner, and I don't have boyfriends, as you know very well," I told him as I sat comfortably on the couch with him.

"Darling, I think you should start dating, live your life a little," he said.

"I tried but that didn't work out. He broke my heart. All boys are jerks," I said.

"Okay, but I'll tell you something, sweetie. Everyone has their own soulmates, but it takes time to find them. Once you do, your heart will begin to beat faster, and no matter what the situation is, he will always be able to make you laugh, and you will feel comfortable with him and he will always protect you no matter what," my father said.

"Well, dad, your bedtime story sucks," I said, laughing along with him.

"and then see how I'll never stop teasing you," he said.

I had tears streaming down my cheeks when I woke up. I missed my father so much. He will never see me with a boyfriend and will never get to taunt me.

"Al, your friends have come to see you," my mother called from downstairs.

"Coming, mom!" I said as I quickly wiped my face and went downstairs.

"Hey hi, so um.. what happened?" I asked after I saw Luke and Lucy waiting for me.

"Al, we are leaving today. Did you forget?" Lucy asked.

"Oh god! Give me ten minutes to get ready," I said and ran back to my room.

Once all my bags were packed, I bid my mom goodbye and got into Luke's car. Poppy and Lucy were coming with Adrian. We drove for two hours in silence. We were enjoying the tranquillity between us.

"So Al, what do you want to do after we get to my place?" Luke asked, breaking the silence in the car.

"Can we go out for dinner? Or maybe hang out with the rest of our friends?" I asked him.

"I think we can go out for dinner. There are a few places that I know that would be great for a romantic getaway," Luke suggested and slowly placed his left hand on mine drawing patterns on my thigh. An involuntary shudder went down my spine so I gently pushed his hand away.

"I think we can go out on a romantic dinner some other time. And maybe this time we can go out with all our friends," I suggested with a bright smile on my face. I saw Luke clench the steering wheel so tight and after that an awkward silence fell in the car. It was kind of disturbing for me.

"Luke, are you okay?" I asked him nervously, breaking the silence between us. And the moment he heard that, the car came to an abrupt stop and he turned around to look at me.

"Are you seriously asking me that? Do I look okay to you, Alina? How long do you expect me to wait for you to take some time out for me, for us?" Luke asked with a fury that made me visibly wither in fear.

"Luke, you should try to understand that I am new to all this," I said, trying to defend. Luke let out a humourless chuckle which nearly brought tears to my eyes. I held them back because I never wanted him to know that I was feeling weak.

"New! I don't think that is the reason, Alina. The real reason is that you don't love me enough to spend some time with me," Luke seethed and it made my heart tighten. This is the only guy in my entire life that I fell in love with and he is insulting me and my feelings. I felt tears leaving my eyes but I quickly wiped them off.

"I think you are right Luke. I never loved you and I can never fall in love with a vile person like you," I said and I saw his face change from anger to disappointment but those emotions vanished as soon as they came.

"I thought so. Anyway, I think it would be best if we break up since I don't want to continue a relationship where I have no importance," Luke said, and I felt like I had been repeatedly stabbed in my chest. This is the reason I had always stopped myself from falling in love because, in the end, all boys are the same.

"So I think it is in our best interests that we break up anyway," I said, and my face was devoid of any emotion.

"I think it is best if we don't tell this to our friends right now. We will let them know after the trip," Luke said and I just nodded my head. After a few more minutes the car started moving again and within no time we reached the house where we had planned to stay.

After unloading my bags from the car, I made my way to the guest room with the help of a housekeeper while Luke went to his. After I was done unpacking, I washed my face and then went downstairs to grab a cup of coffee. When I entered the kitchen I saw that Poppy was there so I quickly greeted her before making myself a cup of coffee.

While I was pouring the coffee into a cup, I felt a pair of hands snake through my waist which made me freeze knowing whose hands they were.

"Act natural," Luke murmured into my ear and gently pulled me towards his rock-hard body, but this time the feeling felt foreign and I felt disgusted to be touched by him but then I kept my mouth shut from saying anything that I would later regret.

"Oh, look at that Pop. Aren't they cute?" I heard Adrian's voice.

"They are really cute together but you don't go and jinx that," Poppy warned.

"I am sure that you two do more than this so I don't think this is anywhere cute," Luke said while removing his hand from my waist and taking a seat on a stool.

"We indeed do more than this but always remember, small things matter the most and those are the things that we cherish. It can be a kiss or a small hug," Adrian said.

"I think I will agree with you on that," Luke said.

You are one of the worst liars that I have ever seen Luke. And you disgust me to the very core.

"Alina, are you alright?" Poppy enquired, bringing me back from my thoughts. I gave her a sweet smile before taking a seat next to Luke.

"I am perfectly fine. I am just having a slight headache, that is all," I reassured her.

"Anyway, Alina and I are going to be upstairs. She said that she wanted some help in sorting out her clothes so I guess I will see you two later." Luke said and got up from the stool while I did the same and followed him out of the kitchen.

"Have fun guys and don't get too noisy." I heard Adrian joke. After we reached the foyer Luke turned around to face me.

"I have a few important things to take care of so I will head out now." Luke said and I nodded. Once I went inside my room, I couldn't help but remember all the moments I had spent with Luke. The carnival, the Ball, everything. I almost froze thinking everything that had just happened. I was so lost that I didn't realize when Poppy came into my room.

"What happened, Ally? You don't seem happy at all, and where the hell is Luke? I thought you made that excuse so both of you could spend some time together," she said, and I was just standing there like a statue, not able to hear anything. I felt Poppy shake me and made me turn towards her.

"You better tell me what is going on. I am your best friend, right? Best friends don't keep secrets, I swear I won't tell anyone," she said, causing me to sob again. I hugged Poppy and cried for long before I could collect myself and tell her what had happened. She didn't know what to say after she heard how Luke broke up with me.

"Ally, you sure that he wasn't joking when he said this and he might ambush you later?" She tried to be sure.

"No Pop, he was not...and I think he is right. I didn't give him my full attention. I was distracted with my schoolwork and everything," I replied.

"Just shut up, Ally! That is one hell of a pathetic excuse to break up with someone you really love. I have never given Adrian my undivided attention, and he has never asked for it. He always told me to concentrate on my studies, make new friends, and enjoy life, and that he will always be there waiting for me, well that is what true love is Ally," she yelled. She literally screamed the last sentence out.

"Maybe what you both have is strong because...you know," I didn't want to say it out loud.

"Rubbish Ally, we didn't have sex for almost a year after we started dating and Adrian never pushed me to. Even when I was ready, he asked me atleast a million times," Poppy explained while I stood there silent, not knowing what else to say.

"Pop, I think I'm really overwhelmed after all this," I said, tired.

"Sure Ally, but if you need anything give me a call and I will be here before you even know," Poppy said.

"Sure thanks Pop for being with me tonight. I don't know what I would do without you," I said.

"Always remember you are not alone in this world. You have people called friends who you can go to when you feel lonely. We will never judge you, Ally, trust me. Stop keeping things bottled up. Spill them out, be it sorrow or happiness, because if you don't you might end up losing yourself into the darkness," Poppy said while hugging me. She pulled back, stared at me for a few seconds and then placed a kiss on my forehead. She then left the room, closing the door behind her.

I think she is right because I do feel like I am being consumed by the darkness slowly every single day. I may look happy outside but inside I am broken into billions of pieces and no one can really put them together.

I sometimes think my dad should have never given me so much love if he had to leave so soon.

I can still remember all the piggyback rides he used to take me on. Whenever my mom scolded me he was always the first one to take a stand. I feel like there is no one to protect me anymore. I know I have friends but that can't be compared to the relationship me and my dad had. Before I could tell him what I want, he used to buy me those things. Life after him has been so different. I sometimes feel it should have been me and not him to leave the world. I was feeling helpless thinking all this when my phone rang.

"Hello," I said.

"Al, hi. Were you crying? You don't sound your usual self." It was Liam and I wanted to end the call so he wouldn't know I wasn't fine, but his voice was making me feel better and it was calming me down.

"No Liam, nothing is wrong. Why did you call?" I asked him, not really answering his question.

"I was thinking if we could hang out and have dinner tonight," he said.

"Sure, that sounds great," I replied.

"Oh okay, I will come and pick you up in half an hour. Can you text me the address?" He asked in a very excited tone.

"Will surely do. See you later."

"Bye, Al!" He said and ended the call. I thought having Liam as a companion would make me feel better so I got off my bed to get ready.

When I was in the kitchen I heard the doorbell ring. I quickly went to open the door.

"Hi, you look nice," Liam said.

"Thanks, shall we leave?" I asked, giving him a little smile.

"Sure, come on." We went towards his car. I noticed that Luke's car was missing.

He must be regretting what he told me and maybe he went for a drive to properly think over it.

Once we hit the road, I texted Poppy that I was out with Liam and will be back home later.

"So where do you want to have dinner?" He asked.

"How would I know this? It is the first time I have come to Scotland," I replied.

"Oh, okay. No problem. I thought since your mom was born and raised here, you might be familiar with the place," he replied.

"We never really came here as my mom's family moved to America long back," I said.

"Oh right, and I wanted to tell you this for quite some time but we were not really on good terms. I am really sorry about your dad," he said.

"Thank you," I said, giving him a sad smile .

After around twenty minutes of drive, we arrived at a restaurant. We went inside and ordered our food, talked a little till it came. The food looked delicious.

"Oh my god! This was like the best dinner ever," I said once we were done.

"I told you this place is great," Liam said.

"Yeah, so can we have dessert now? I am craving some Choco lava cake" I said.

"Why don't we go have that at the dessert shop a few blocks from here. They have a variety there," he said.

"No, let's just have it here. I can't go to a different place now. I am really tired," I replied.

"Fine," he said and ordered the desserts.

While we were waiting for our desserts, I saw a familiar figure coming inside the restaurant. I took a closer look. I knew who it was and it felt like someone had poured ice-cold water over my head, it was none other than...

21

LUKE! It was Luke, and he had a girl next to him, and while he was waiting for the waitress to get them a seat, he kissed her on the lips right there, and I felt like my entire world had come crashing down all over again.

How could he do that to me. It has been 24 hours since we broke up, and he was already with another girl? I think I should have listened to Liam and had dessert somewhere else so I did not have to see this.

I couldn't speak and my vision began to blur because my eyes started brimming with tears. I heard Liam's voice asking a question from afar, so I quickly cleared my mind and tried to listen.

"Al, is that Luke with another girl there?" He asked angrily.

"I know, I didn't know that love is so unpredictable," I replied.

"Is he cheating on you?" He asked, his face full of concern.

"No Liam, we officially broke up just a couple of hours ago. I mean he broke up with me. I begged him not to and now I realise what a fool I was to fall for him," I said, still looking at Luke, unable to contain the tears. They started streaming down my face.

"Al, let's get out of here. You can tell me everything later," Liam said and stood up to leave.

We made our way to the exit passing Luke and unfortunately, he saw us.

"Al, you are here…" He was about to say something but I couldn't take it so I stopped him from saying anything.

"Don't, Luke! I didn't know that you were so desperate to leave. Now I know that you never really loved me. I being the fool I am, thought that you loved me as much as I did and that you just wanted some time to think about your actions but you proved me wrong," I said, giving a humorous laugh.

"Al, I was.."

"Just shut up, Luke! Don't you think you have lied enough? Please don't even show your face ever again, it disgusts me," I said, raising my pitch. I felt tears running down my cheek so I just ran out of the place. I was standing near Liam's car when he came and hugged me, that made me sob even more. I held him tight and cried my heart out.

"Are you okay now?" He asked and I somehow managed to control myself to look at him.

"Thank you for being here, Liam," I replied.

"I will always be here, Al. Now care to explain to me what that asshole did to you," he said. I nodded and explained everything to him.

"Al, I wanted to warn you about this last week but you never wanted me to talk about Luke," he said.

"So did you already know that Luke was cheating on me?" I asked, surprised.

"No, I did not know that, but I knew Luke is not someone you should give your heart to. I just found out last week who that unknown number was," he said. I was eager to know who it was. I wanted to know who destroyed Liam's and Lucy's friendship.

"Liam? Who was it?" I asked.

For a few minutes, Liam just stared at the floor and didn't react before slowly replying.

"Luke," he said.

"What? Why would he do that? I thought he and Lucy were friends," I said, completely shocked.

"They are friends but Luke and I are not. He wanted to take a kind of revenge on me," Liam said.

"REVENGE ON WHAT, LIAM?" I asked, shouting at him.

"It all started back in our freshman year when we were all very good friends: Adrian, Poppy, Lucy and I. There was one more person, Madison, Luke's girlfriend. She was very friendly to us but at the same time she was really mean and snobby to others. She was very rich, just like Luke, and they were in a very serious relationship. I never really liked her personally. Whenever Luke wasn't around, she would annoy me by flirting with me. I told her to back off several times but she never listened. One day we all had a party at my house and I got very drunk. I couldn't stay awake for long so I headed back to my room to sleep. I didn't know that Madison was following me. When I told her to leave, she kissed me and I was too drunk to push her away. When I realised she had removed her top, I quickly tried to push her but at that very moment, Luke entered my room. When he saw us, I tried to explain, but he punched me in the face and stormed out, with Madison following him. The next day, I tried to explain what had happened, but Madison had convinced them that I had forced her to sleep with me, and no one believed me, so our friendship broke. After a few months, Madison broke up with him and went to Australia. Since then Luke never got into a serious relationship."

"So Luke still thinks that you cheated on him with his girlfriend?" I asked and he said yes.

I should have listened to Liam before. I could have saved myself from this heartbreak.

"Do you want to go home now?" Liam asked.

"Yes but not to Luke's. I don't really want to see him again. Is it okay if we go to your place?" I asked.

"Yeah, sure. No problem at all," he replied. I texted Poppy that I won't be returning that night, switched off my phone and got inside the car. I wanted to be away from everything for a while.

We finally arrived at Liam's house after a very long drive.

"So, who all stay here with you?" I asked him once he parked his car in the driveway.

"Two of my best friends, Mike and Evan," he replied.

"Don't worry, they are awesome! You will love them," Liam said.

"Oh, cool. So shall we go inside?" I asked.

"Sure, c'mon in," he said and we made our way into the house, through the front door. I was surprised to see how beautiful it looked. It was not a mansion like Luke's, but a modern house with glass walls that allows one to see the snowfall and bright moonlight outside.

"Hey man, where were you? You left without informing," someone said, coming out of the living room.

"And who is this?" Asked the guy with dirty blonde hair and dark eyes.

"Mike, this is Alina. Alina, this is my stupid best friend Mike," Liam said.

"Hello, nice meeting you," I said, extending my hand for a handshake.

"Hello, Cutie! nice meeting you too," Mike said with a grin.

"Yeah, I forgot to tell you Al, he's a big flirt, so unless you want to start something with him, I suggest you stay away," Liam said sarcastically.

"Oh, that's not fair, Beanie," Mike said, "At least give the girl a chance."

"Anyway Mike, where is Evan?" Liam asked.

"He is out with his girlfriend. I won't be surprised if he doesn't come back tonight," Mike said, and then he turned to me and asked the most absurd question.

"Hey cutie, what is your full name?"

"Uh..Alina Campbell why do you ask?" I asked, puzzled.

"oh so you are that g…"

"Mike, I thought you said you have a game to watch tonight?" Liam interjected.

"Oh, right! I totally forgot about that." He left the room leaving me and Liam alone.

"What was Mike trying to say?" I inquired.

"Nothing, he's just a little out of his mind sometimes," Liam said nervously

"But I th..."

"Let me take you to the guest room, it's already late, and you must be tired," Liam said, pushing me towards the stairs.

"So, what do you think?" He asked as he opened the door to the guest room.

It was a very beautiful and comfortable space.

"Thank you, Liam! I think it's great," I replied.

"I'm glad you liked it. Okay, then. Good night, Al! If you need anything, I'll be in the room next door," he replied.

"Yeah okay, and Liam, do you have any clothes because I didn't think of bringing anything with me?" I asked.

"Yeah sure, but I don't know if you'd like them. I mean they are all my clothes," Liam said, laughing.

"I really don't mind," I smiled.

"Okay settle down while I bring something for you," he said and left the room.

Liam's POV

I was furious when Al told me about her breakup with Luke. I knew Luke was a jerk but I thought he really loved Al after Madison. I was devastated when I saw Al cry on my chest because I knew how much she must have loved him. I felt guilty at the same time because if I had told her about Luke's true nature when I had the chance, I believe I could have stopped this from happening.

"Hello, are you manufacturing clothes for me?" My chain of thoughts was broken by Al's sweet voice.

"Sorry, I was just zoned out...um...and here you go," I said nervously, extending one of my black tee-shirts and grey sweatpants toward her.

"I hope this will be ok with you," I said.

"Yeah, they are great, and thank you again, Liam, for listening to me tonight," she said.

"No problem Al, what are friends for?" I said with a smile. Honestly, I wanted to tell her how much I wish for her to be more than friends and that I'll never hurt her.

"Good night, then," she said, planting a kiss on my cheek, that made me blush. I turned red.

"Oh, how cute you look when you blush! Okay, bye!" She said and left the room. For a moment, I froze where I was standing.

Alina's POV

After returning back to my room, I still had a huge smile plastered on my face thinking about what I just did. After dwelling on that for quite some time I took Liam's clothes with me to the washroom. After a hot shower I laid down on my bed and took a book from my nightstand to read. I was so engrossed in the reading that I didn't hear my phone ringing. I answered the call.

"Hi Alina, where are you?" I heard Luke' frantic voice from the other end which made me want to break my phone.

"What do you want, Luke?" I asked him.

"Al, I know you're upset, but please hear me out. I didn't cheat on you if that's what you're thinking. I agree, I saw Maya a few weeks ago, but I was waiting before we broke up to start a relationship with her," he explained.

"Well, Luke, thank you for explaining yourself; if you're done, then I'll now sleep," I said.

"Why didn't you come home?" he asked.

"I am safe and protected Luke and I won't be returning. Thank you for asking," I said and hung up before he could say something more. I then went back to sleep, putting my phone on the nightstand.

I woke up at the sound of my phone. I discovered it was Poppy.

"What's up, Pop?" I inquired.

"Currently, the blue sky with the sun is up here," she sarcastically replied.

"Yes, Pop, very amusing. So, why did you call?" I asked.

"Where are you, Al?" She sounded concerned.

"I'm at Liam's place, don't worry, I'll be there later," I told her.

"Oh, fine, and we're going skiing after lunch, so be back by then," she said.

"Yes, Pop."

"Bye, take care," she said as she hung up the phone.

I slowly got out of bed and went to the washroom to freshen up before going down for breakfast.

22

Liam's POV

When I got down I saw Mike sitting in the kitchen.

"Hey, good morning, Mike!" I said as I made my way to the fridge to get some milk.

"Good morning, Beanie!" Mike said cheerfully.

"Would you mind not calling me that in front of Alina, please?" I asked as I started making myself a cup of coffee.

"Oh, hey, why don't you tell her you like her? Now that she has broken up with that jerk face, don't you think you should?" Mike asked.

"No Mike, she doesn't like me that way so you better stop contemplating," I gave him a stare.

"Come on, man! Why don't you just tell her and let her decide?" He exclaimed.

"Tell me what?" Al asked and I froze in my place.

"Urgh...Mike here wanted to...um," I started, but Mike interrupted.

"What he was going to tell you was that we are staying in Scotland until the New Year so we thought you might want to stay with us and celebrate. Trust me it will be really fun," Mike said.

I got confused because I thought Mike wanted to go home next week as he had plans of going to Cambridge where the three of us generally celebrate New Year.

"That sounds fun. I will definitely think about it and let you know. Liam, is that coffee you are making? Can I have some?" Al asked.

"Sure," I said as I poured coffee in two mugs and turned to offer it to her, and then I saw her wearing my clothes. I got goosebumps all over my body, she looked so cute in that oversized tee-shirt and sweatpants.

"Hello, I know your clothes look awkward on me, but you don't have to make it too plain by staring at me like that," she said with a cute pout.

"Hey cutie, no need to think you look ugly in those clothes because honestly you look horrible," Mike said, laughing. When I saw Al, her face had turned red from embarrassment. She grabbed a cushion from the sofa and threw it at Mike, hitting him hard on the face.

"Are you training yourself in martial arts or what?" Mike whined.

"That will remind you to never tease me," Al said, smiling.

"Oh, you are so dead now," Mike said with a wicked smile. He quickly rose from his stool and began chasing Al, and I stood there laughing at their silly fight.

"PLEASE LIAM, SAVE ME FROM THIS INSANELY STUPID FRIEND OF YOURS," Al begged.

"Okay Mike, that's enough. You can get your revenge another time. Leave her alone," I said.

"No way, now you're in trouble too man," he said, so I grabbed Al's hand and ran into the living room with Mike chasing us.

At one point, Mike threw something at my leg, causing me to topple and fall on my back with Al on top of me. When I looked at her, I saw her staring back at me with those huge green eyes, and I slowly moved my gaze to her lush pink lips, then back to her eyes. We were just a few inches apart. I was breathing fast and I could feel her heart pounding against me.

Alina's POV

"PLEASE LIAM SAVE ME FROM THIS INSANELY STUPID FRIEND OF YOURS," I begged.

"Okay Mike, that's enough. You can get your revenge another time. Leave her alone," he said now smiling at Mike.

"No way, now you're in trouble too man," Mike said.

Then Liam just grabbed my hand and ran into the living room, with Mike chasing us. At one point, I saw Mike throw something at Liam's leg, causing him to topple and fall on his back, with me landing on top of him. When I looked at him, he was staring at me intently with those midnight blue eyes, and then his gaze slowly moved to my lips, then back to my eyes. We were just a few feet apart. My breathing hitched as was his and I could feel his heart beating very fast against me.

"Hey Liam, why are you on the carpet with your girlfriend. your room isn't that far, you know?" Someone teased, and I snapped out of my stupor and scrambled from atop Liam to stand up, and he, too, quickly got up and stood next to me.

"Oh hey Evvy, when did you get home and that… that isn't my girlfriend. She is just a friend," Liam said.

"Got here just a few minutes ago," Evan said. "So, you must be Alina Campbell. Nice to meet you," he turned to me, giving me a charming smile.

"Yes, hi! How do you know me?" I asked.

"Should I tell you the truth ?" He joked.

"I think the truth would suffice," I replied.

"Well, I go to the same school as you," he said with a grin.

"But that's really not the reason why I know you. Actually, Liam has talked a lot about you," he said.

I looked at him confused.

"Al, this is Evan Martin," Liam said.

"Ervamatin? Your parents named you after hair oil," I said, teasing him.

"I know you heard my name properly, Punkin," he said laughing.

"What the hell does Punkin mean?" I asked.

"It means stubborn," he said.

"Enough, you both! C'mon let's have breakfast now," Liam interrupted.

I should quickly have my breakfast as I need to leave and head back to Luke's for skiing.

"So Al, are you staying with us for the new year celebrations?" Liam inquired, his gaze fixed on the road.

"I've been thinking about that because me and my friends will be leaving in two days and then we'll go to Boardwalk for the new year celebrations," he said.

That was our initial plan before I saw Luke sucking faces with a random girl not even 24 hours after our breakup. If I go now, I'll have to see him with his new girlfriend and I don't really want to see his face.

"Al, I think I asked a very simple question. You can answer with a 'yes' or a 'no'. What are you calculating," he said, bringing me back from my thoughts.

"Yes," I replied.

"Does that mean you're staying with?" he inquired, his face thoughtful.

"Yes, I'm staying with you guys," I said, smiling.

"But I have to tell you something, we could have official dinners where some extra people can come to my place and hang out too," he said now with a big grin on his face.

When I heard what he said, my face fell. I completely forgot Liam has a girl.

Why am I feeling dejected? Liam isn't my boyfriend or anything; he's just a friend. I should stop being stupid and protect my heart this time.

"So, um...will your girlfriend be coming to the new year party to hang out with us?" I nervously inquired.

"Oh no, we broke up. It was mutual so we are still friends. She has gone to celebrate New Year and Christmas with her grandparents in Australia so she won't be visiting us," he replied.

I turned around and grinned at him as well. I was now confused who else would join.

"Yeah, you know Evan's girlfriend and the girl that Mike hangs out with may join us," he said.

"Wait, were my thoughts that loud?" I questioned.

"I am sure they were," he answered, and I groaned.

"You know you look cute when you groan," Liam said, laughing. I turned around and grinned at him.

"I'll call you so you can come pick me up," I told Liam as I exited the car.

“Sure, bye Al, take care,” he said.

“You too,” I said, waving my hand as he walked away from Luke's house. When I entered the kitchen, Luke was standing there with a mug in his hand, and when I saw him, I became enraged.

“Al, can we talk? Please?” He begged.

“I think we have already talked and sorted everything out last night, Luke. if you can remember,” I said, annoyed.

“Al, I know you are mad bu...”

“Wow, Luke! You found out I was mad. I will give you your award later,” I said, giving him a fake smile.

“Al, why don't you listen to me? Fine, I accept I cheated but you cheated too with...Liam,” he said emphasising more on the last word.

“We are just friends and that is all, we were not kissing behind your back,” I said.

“Then why were you on a date with him last night?” He asked.

“I was no....”

“Hey guys, what is going on here? Looks like both of you are going to rip off each other's throat,” Adrian said while coming into the kitchen.

“Um....no man we were just arguing on what to eat. Right Al?” Luke said, now placing his hand on my shoulder and pulling me closer to him .

I got really mad now and I yanked his hand off my shoulder and shouted at him.

“WE ARE OFFICIALLY OVER, LUKE. I HATE YOU SO MUCH! STOP PRETENDING. YOU HAVE ALREADY

BROKEN ME INTO BITS A..AND P...P..PI...PIECES," I screamed with tears flowing down my face and then I turned and ran into my room.

I crawled into my bed and pulled the comforter over my head and started crying.

Why do I have to go through this heartbreak, why can't I have a normal life with no complications? If my dad was here, he would have comforted me, protected me. Why did he have to leave...

"Ally, are you alright?" I heard Adrian ask me softly.

I slowly pulled my comforter away from me and tried to sit. Adrian quickly hugged me.

"Ally, please stop crying. I heard what happened between you and Luke. Pops told me just now. Why didn't you share this with us before? We would have helped you and been there," said Adrian.

"I want… to t..talk to my d...dad," I said and started crying again.

"Shall I call him?" He asked.

"No, he travels a lot. He can't talk. Anyway, can we go skiing?" I tried hard to change the subject.

"Sure, we'll do whatever you want. Quickly get ready, okay?" He gave a comforting smile.

23

Poppy, Lucy and I went with Adrian to the skiing resort. It looked like Luke's new girlfriend was going to stick around with us just like I had predicted. After my outburst, it was final that Luke and I weren't going to date anymore. Luke tried explaining the situation to my friends, saying that it was not his fault, but no one bought his words. He was hanging out with his new girlfriend, Rachel. She tried talking to me, but I ignored her. Well, in her defense, she is bolder and way modern than I could be, her dressing sense is impeccable, to the point where it sometimes seems unnecessary. To top it all off, she has blond hair and magnetic blue eyes that seem to draw people towards her by just giving them a glance.

I didn't want my friends to avoid him because of my personal problems so I convinced them to be more polite towards him and stop worrying about me. That didn't work at first, but it did later after I blackmailed them, saying that if they give Luke the cold shoulder because of me, I'm cutting all ties with them. I didn't think it would work, but it did, and it now seemed that they love and care for me as well.

"Hello guys, I think you're late," Luke said with a smile on his face

"We should take our sweet time to come here right? Is there a problem with that?" Adrian asked once we arrived at the resort and put on our skiing equipment before heading outside to the skiing section.

“No, there isn't any, I'm glad you guys made it here,” he said now, clearly sensing the tension.

“So Rosal?” Poppy inquired.

“It's Rachel,” she corrected.

“Okay, don't care what it is, now tell me how did you guys meet?” Poppy inquired.

“We met two weeks ago at a coffee shop, actually it was so cute, I went there with my friends and as I was taking my drinks to my table, and we bumped into each other,” she said in a dreamy voice and after hearing her my blood started boiling.

“Oh, Alina. Don't worry. We didn't date behind your back, I swear. I am not that kind of a girl who steals someone's boyfriend,” she quickly added when she saw my face had turned red with anger.

“I don't care what you do,” I said in a stern voice and left. I was there to enjoy skiing and not for these things.

Two days later...

“Ally, please come celebrate the New Year with us; I guarantee the cat lady will not join us,” Poppy said.

“No, Pops. You know I need some time to put myself together before I leave for home,” I said.

“Sure. Then take care, alright? And don't forget to call and update me on what is going on.”

“Sure. Bye,” I said, and she hugged me before leading me to Liam's car.

“Hey Punkin, you came!” Evan said as I entered Liam's house.

"Yeah, I came, thank you for asking," I replied with a smile.

"Hey, come on Al, I'll show you the bed, and dinner will be served shortly. And we're having a bonfire tonight, can you join us?" Liam asked.

"Why not, that would be fun in this cold whether," I replied.

"Well, we'll have that after dinner and don't forget to wear something warm," he added.

"Sure, thanks Liam for letting me spend some time here with you guys," I told them.

"Al you don't have to thank me for that, you are always welcome here," Liam said.

After dinner Mike and Evan went to the back yard to start the fire while i was in the kitchen helping Liam carry all the drinks and snacks outside.

"Hey cutie, come over here and sit with me, I'll keep you nice and warm better than the fire," Mike said with a grin on his face, so I went over and sat next to him.

"Thanks Mike for the seat, but I think the fire will keep me warm enough," I said, pushing his hand away from my shoulder.

"So guys, who wants beer and who wants vodka?" Evan asked while coming out with his girlfriend.

"Hey Punkin, you don't look like the beer kind. You look like someone who only drinks champagne," Evan said while passing the beer around.

"What makes you think that?" I asked Evan."

"Because you look like some Duchess with the way you sit and the way you carry yourself with poise," he said.

"Well, I guess my mom's etiquette lessons have paid off," I said, grinning.

“I think beer would be perfect by me,” I said as Evan handed me a can.

“Hi, I'm Laura. Evan's girlfriend,” she said as she introduced herself.

“I'm Alina, good to meet you,” I said.

“Same here, you know how pleased I am that at long last another girl has joined this party of pathetic losers with their lame jokes,” she said with a wink.

“Hey Looney, we aren't that bad,” Mike protested, and we all laughed.

“Guys come on, let's play truth or dare,” Mike said and with that all of us got nearer to the fire .

“Everybody, settle down. Let me start first,” Mike said as he sipped his beer.

“Okay Beanie, truth or dare?” He asked Liam.

“Dare,” Liam said.

“Alright! You just have to mix the Vodka and beer in equal proportion in this glass and drink it,” Mike said.

“That is super easy. I never thought you would give me anything as easy as that,” Liam said with a puzzled expression on his face.

Mike simply grinned and passed him a large cup. Liam filled it with vodka and beer, and drank.

“Done,” he said, putting the cup back on the floor after a few minutes.

“ Well, now it's my turn,” Evan said. “Punkin, truth or dare?” He asked me.

“Reality,” I replied because I didn't want to do a dare too fast.

"You are taking the easy route out but okay," he said with a smirk and that made me nervous.

"Punkin, who did you lose your V - card to?" Evan asked.

"Um....I....a....I.." I stammered because, truth be told, I still had my v-card, but I didn't know how to admit that.

You can do it, Al! Don't care what they think of you, just spit it out.. " "I'm still a virgin," I confidently proclaimed as I quickly sipped from my beer, not wanting to see their reactions.

"WHAT? ARE YOU SERIOUS?" Evan asked as beer flew from his mouth and landed on the fire, causing it to flare up even further.

"Cutie, are you serious?" Mike inquired, his face flushed with confusion.

"I thought you were dating Luke and something might have happened between you too," Mike said.

"He tried to persuade me to join him to bed, but I wasn't ready," I explained.

"Why is that cutie?" Mike inquired, sounding perplexed.

"Actually Mike, it is not your turn to ask questions and I have already answered mine," I replied.

"Fine, let's move on." He finally let the subject slide away.

Two hours later, everything and everyone had gone crazier. Mike was drenched in icy water. Evan was dressed in a newspaper outfit. Liam was more drunk than all of us. The vodka and beer combination had taken its toll on him.

"Cutie, truth or dare?" Mike asked.

"Dare," I answered.

"Oh great, now I'll blindfold you and turn you around a few times, and whoever you land on, you must kiss him hard and raw for 2 minutes, but if you land on our dear Loony, you must sleep on the sofa tonight with no blankets," Mike said.

"Okay, I'm ready. I hope I end up kissing Laura. Sleeping on the couch would be better than kissing these idiots," I said.

"Alright, come on everyone! let's get away from the fire for safety" Mike said and all of us went away and formed a circle, I stood at the centre. Evan blindfolded me with a cloth.

"Ready or not, Punkin? I am now going to spin you around," he said

"Okay" I replied, and Evan began spinning me. He returned to his spot and I continued spinning. A few moments later I came to a halt and started walking straight. I collided with something hard.

When I opened my blindfold all I saw was a pair of midnight blue eyes staring down at me.

"Okay Punkin you found your Romeo now why don't you kiss him Mike will start the timer," Evan said.

I looked at Liam, his lips were pink and lush. He slowly leaned in towards me, I closed my eyes and leaned towards him. When our lips met, a jolt of electricity shot through my body. Liam slowly wrapped his hands around my waist and pulled me closer, so close that there was no space between us, and I wrapped my hand around his neck. When his hand moved from my waist to my lower back, I gasped. He kissed me harder and the butterflies in my stomach intensified. I had never felt this way with anyone before.

" Alright love birds, that's enough. I think we've had enough of seeing you two suck each other's faces," Evan said, and I quickly pulled away from Liam and stood a few feet away from him. My breathing was now really rapid and my heart was pounding. We were still looking at each other. Before he could say something, we wriggled away.

A couple of hours later we were all very exhausted, so we decided to go back inside. Evan and Laura went to Evan's room, and Mike crashed on the sofa. I saw Liam stumbling up the staircase and making his way to his room. I went into the kitchen and drank some water before heading back to my room. When I went in and turned on the light, I saw Liam sleeping on my bed. I tried to wake him up but he did not move.

“Good night, Liam,” I said softly, knowing that he was fast asleep. I put some pillows between us and turned to sleep on my side.

24

Liam's POV

Oh, man! I shouldn't have drank so much last night. It feels like my head will explode.

I couldn't recall a thing I did the other night. I sat down and poured a glass of water for me to drink. I couldn't even open my eyes. While drinking water I suddenly remembered something.

Mike gave Al a dare and then... I KISSED HER.

WAIT WAIT WAIT WAIT I kissed Al.

It was surreal. When her lips touched mine, a wave of electricity ran through my body. Every time she touched me, my soul lit up. It was the best kiss I'd ever had..

But then I realised I shouldn't have kissed her. We were just friends and she had recently broken up with Luke. I decided I should talk to her because I didn't want to lose her confidence in me again. I tried getting out of bed and then suddenly I felt someone's toe touching mine. It took me some time to register and to comprehend that Al was sleeping next to me, snoring lightly. She looked like an angel.

Why is she here? How did she end up in my room?

I looked around, walls painted in cream colour, a glass window on one side. This was not my room. It was Al's. I might have crashed in here last night, I thought to myself.

It would be better for me to leave before she wakes up. I'll explain everything to her later.

As I was about to get out of bed, I heard Al stirring in her sleep.

"Liam...," she said in a sleepy tone.

After a few moments she was wide awake.

"How the hell am I on the right side of the bed? I was sleeping on the left side and had a wall of pillows in between..." she blabbered and turned to her right to see that her wall of pillows had collapsed.

"Sorry I roll a lot in my sleep," she said.

"That's fine. Why didn't you tell me to go back to my room and sleep?" I inquired. She stared at me before responding.

"I tried to wake you up many times but you wouldn't move," she said.

"Oh, I am so sorry," I apologised.

" That's fine, and, don't worry about last night's kiss, it's fine too. We're still friends," she said before I could even ask.

I felt relieved that she did not regret kissing me.

Alina's POV

I don't know why I feel safe with him. I felt so comfortable sleeping next to him.

After Liam left, I took a shower and went down to have breakfast. I was feeling fresh and did not have a hangover as I had not drunk much the other night. When I walked into the kitchen, I saw Mike and Liam sitting having coffee.

"Hi guys, how are your heads?" I asked as I poured myself a cup.

"It's the worst, cutie, I'm never drinking that much again," Mike said.

"Oh Mike, you poor soul!" I said with a sarcastic laugh.

"Hey Al, shall we go out today?" Liam asked.

"Sure, where are we going?"

"I was thinking of going camping, the weather looks so good today," he replied.

"Sure, that sounds interesting. I'll get ready and come," I said.

"How much longer?" I asked Liam.

"Just a couple of hours," he replied.

"This is what you've been saying for the past one hour," I grumbled.

"Oh wait, we're almost there," he said.

"Fine."

"Come on Al, live a little. If you smile for me, the world won't end," he said, smirking.

When we arrived, there were already a few cars parked in the parking lot.

"I think not everyone likes hiking," I remarked putting on my backpack.

"Most of the people come here for skiing and miss out on all the fun," he said. "Let's head to the main office before we start."

We were all set to hike and the beginning was tough.

"Al," Liam called after hiking for an hour in silence.

"Yes?" I asked.

"Um.. Luke called asking how you were holding up. He said you didn't pick up any of his calls and that he was concerned about you," Liam said.

"Liam, next time that asshole calls tell him that Alina is no longer in his life and he should stop pretending that he cares." I was fuming with anger and I started walking fast, ahead of Liam. He tried to stop me but I continued walking.

I came to a halt near a tree to catch my breath when Liam ran up to me.

"What is it?" I asked rather rudely.

"Al, we're on the wrong track," he said, panting.

"Oh, no! I'm so sorry, come on, let's go back, we can follow back our footprints," I said, and Liam nodded.

As we tried heading back, snow began to fall. We had to stop where we were. We waited for an hour but it didn't stop. It started increasing more.

"I think we should just build a tent and stop here till the snow stops" Liam suggested.

I felt that was a good idea so we started building the tent. It took us about thirty minutes to do that. It started getting colder and darker outside.

"Do you have the sticks we collected earlier?" Liam asked.

"Yes," I said and we went outside to light a fire.

This is all my fault. I shouldn't have let my temper get the better of me. Now we can get help only in the morning.

Liam started a fire to keep us warm. I took the food from my backpack and went outside the tent.

"Liam, do we have enough water?" I asked.

"Yes, I think it will be enough for the day," he replied.

"Oh. That is good, and did you try contacting anyone?" I asked.

"No luck Al, I think if we start moving in the morning we might get something," he said.

"You are right, but I'm worried. Won't there be snakes or something at this time of night?" I asked, terrified. "What if some snake comes and swallows me whole? I haven't even been to Bermuda yet."

"Don't worry, I won't let you die too soon, and if you like, we can go to Bermuda in the summer," Liam said laughing at me.

"Wait, were my thoughts that loud?" I inquired, perplexed.

"Loud and clear cupcake," he replied.

"Here you go, the food is ready," Liam said as he carried the food into the tent.

I grabbed the food from him and began eating as if I hadn't eaten for days.

"Come on Al, you eat like a bear who has just come out of hibernation," he said.

"Shut up and eat your food before I eat it."

After we had finished eating, we put the garbage in a bag and got ready for bed.

"Li-li I want to pee," I said, making a baby face at him.

"Li-li? Who is that?" Liam asked me, confusion written all over his face. "That's what I'm going to call you from now! Now can we hurry up? I really need to pee!" I whined.

" "Fine, come on," he said, and we began walking until we came to a halt near a bush.

“ You pee here. I’ll look on the other side,” Liam said, pointing to the bush.

“Liam, you're nuts, I can't pee in a bush, I'm not a caveman like you. Let's go find a toilet,” I said, and began moving away.

“Ally bear, we might have found a camping site if we had followed the trail, but you had to storm out in the wrong direction, so now we will have to rely on primitive methods to survive,” he said trying to stop me.

“Fine...” I said and went behind the bush to pee.

We returned to our tent after I finished, and Liam and I crawled into our respective sleeping bags.

“Good night Li-li.”

“Good night, Ally bear.”

I tossed and turned for about an hour but couldn’t fall asleep. It was getting very cold there, so cold that I was shivering. On the other hand, Liam was sleeping very comfortably, that too shirtless.

Doesn't he feel cold? Is he even human?

“ Al, do you want to sleep with me because it looks like you'll freeze to an ice block before the sun comes up?” Liam asked, his voice filled with worry.

“Su...sur...sure,” I replied, trembling.

Liam came out of his sleeping bag and into mine. When our bodies came in contact, I felt a bit of warmth return to me. We still had a small gap between us and Liam's hand was draped over mine. I turned towards Liam to look at his face. I could feel the tension between us. He pulled me closer, we didn’t say a word, just stared at each other for long.

He slowly started drawing circles on my back and I moved so close to him that there was nothing in between. The last thing I saw before I fell asleep were those gorgeous midnight blue eyes and a lot of emotions in them, maybe emotions of love too. I did not know if I was ready to fall, ready to hurt myself again.

When I got up the next morning, Liam was nowhere to be seen. It felt cold, and that reminded me of his smell, his warmth. I realised that I miss him a lot.

Stop it Alina! He is just a friend of yours, nothing else. He also thinks the same way, I am sure.

"Hey, good morning! I made you some breakfast." said Liam when I came out of the tent.

"Thanks!" I said, taking the food from him.

"Let's get moving after breakfast, what do you say?"

"Sounds good to me. Where will we go after this, Li-Li?"

"There is an artificial hot spring near the campsite. We can stay there for a while and then head back home," Liam said walking in front of me.

"Sounds like a plan!" I looked around, the surroundings were beautiful with snow-covered trees. I was wondering how it would all look in the summer with birds singing, waterfall running and animals wandering around.

"Hey Ally Bear, slow down! If you don't watch where you're going, you might end up in a hole and trust me I won't come to save you," Liam said.

"Thanks, I really appreciate it," I moved forward. I suddenly remembered that my dad had said the same thing to me once.

Al, don't cry. You're stronger than that.

Liam understood, he came to me and hugged me. It felt like I had kept so much inside that it was making it hard for me to breathe.

"Every year at this time, my dad and I would go hiking in the snow, and he would always make fun of me. It is also his birthday today. We would make a snowman and..." I couldn't take it anymore and started crying loudly.

I had always held my feelings in check and before this I had never told anybody how much I missed him. I don't know why, but I felt like I could say anything to Liam. It felt like he shielded me from the entire world." Shh Al, do you know something? If you don't let go of the past, the past will never let go of you. Your father has never abandoned you; he is always watching you and wants you to move on with your life. If you're always stuck in the past, you know, he'll be sad. Promise me you'll try to move on," Liam said softly in my ear.

"Li-li, how can I just forget him and move on?" I sobbed.

"Don't forget him, always remember him, he'll always live in your heart. You know Al, your past makes you who you are today. Try being a strong woman and see how your life goes."

"Thanks Liam," I said hugging him tighter.

"Al… I can't breathe," he laughed, both of us laughed.. "This water is boiling hot, I can't get in there," I protested as I stood outside the hot water pool.

"Ally Bear, come on in, I'll hold you. It won't be that hot," he said.

I sat on Liam's lap for a while, he put both his hands around my stomach and pulled me closer. He was right, the water wasn't that hot.

"See, I told you," he said. I guess he was right.

25

Hey Cutie, welcome back! How was camping?" Mike asked.

"Oh, it was fantastic! I had a lot of fun," I replied cheerfully.

Liam entered the house.

"Hey Beanie, Shell came here yesterday looking for you. I told her you would be going back to your home today. She said she would join us for lunch," Mike told him.

"Okay," he replied and went upstairs looking quite annoyed.

"Hey Cutie, would you like to join me for lunch?" He asked.

"But you said some shellfish was coming to lunch today, right?" I asked sarcastically.

"Oh, I hate her, she's a pain in the ass." He looked very irritated.

"Why do you hate her so much?" I was curious to know." "I think you may have heard they dated for about six months before Liam broke it off. She was very manipulative and full of herself. She still desperately tries to get Liam to like her," Mike said.

It was then that I realized Mike was talking about the same girl who had threatened me to stay away from Liam, Shelly. I definitely wanted to see her, and I didn't really have to wait.

"Liam, how cold the winter is without you! I've been missing you terribly," she said to Liam as she entered the house.

She tried hugging him but he gently moved her away. I was trying hard not to laugh and she noticed that.

"So where is Evan and his girlfriend?" She asked.

"They went out for lunch," Mike answered.

"Lunch is ready. Come, let's sit down and eat," Liam said, and we all went to the table.

"So Alina, did your friends leave you because you broke up with Luke?" Shelly asked as we ate.

"I just needed some time to get myself together before school begins," I said flatly.

"Oh, you know, I heard several stories about why you two broke up, but the most believable one was that you are a prude, and that is why Luke left you," she said.

I was fuming with anger.

How dare she call me names?

"Shelly, if she's a prude, what are you, a..." Liam seemed more annoyed than I was.

"Oh, please stop it. You know me better than that," she said, blinking her eyelashes.

"I think you should stop nagging Alina," he warned, and then we ate in silence.." Liam, as it was a last-minute plan to come to Scotland, I didn't book a hotel. Can I stay here?" Shelly inquired.

"I don't.." before he could finish, she interrupted.

"Thank you so much, Liam! It means a lot to me." Shelly stood up to get her luggage.

"Mike, can you please take her to the guest bedroom?" Liam asked, rubbing his temples with his thumb and forefinger.

Mike stood up and showed her the way. Once Shelly left the dining room I fell back on my chair and let out a sigh.

Why does she have to come here of all places!

"Al, I am so sorry. I couldn't stop Shelly from staying here but I give you my word she won't stay here for long. I will go and talk to her," Liam said with a sad face.

"No, it's alright Liam. Let her stay after it will only be for a few days, right? I think as long as I avoid her, I will be fine," I replied before getting up from my chair and heading back to my room. I didn't know how the time flew by but when I came back downstairs to drink water I saw Evan and Rachel were back from their lunch date and I noticed that Rachel had a scowl on her face. That is when I heard the annoying nasal voice again, asking Evan questions. The funny part was that throughout the entire conversation I noticed that Evan was trying so hard not to bash Shelly's head with a vase.

"Hey, you guys! It's been a while since I've seen you," Shelly said.

"Why are you even here?" Evan asked rudely.

"Oh, I am great too Evan, thanks for asking. I am celebrating New Year with you guys," she said happily.

"No one invited you," Evan said coldly.

"I invited myself," she said.

"Hey Al, didn't you tell me that you were going to show me your art work when I got back home?" Evan suddenly asked me and all three pairs of eyes stared at me.

"Uh, I was?" I asked him with a confused look on my face.

"Yes, you were. Now come on," Evan said and dragged Rachel and me upstairs.

Once we were in a nearby room, Evan turned towards me with a grateful look on his face.

" Thank you so much! You came at the right time," Evan said. "You guys hate her, uh?" I joked and Rachel made a funny face.

"We hate her to the moon and back. I have no idea how Liam even dated her," Rachel exclaimed.

"So do you guys want dinner?" I asked .

"No, I am not going down there today. I think we will head back to bed," Evan said and Rachel quickly nodded her head. After that I headed to my room to sleep since I didn't want to see Shelly's face again.

I was sitting on the sofa downstairs while everybody was asleep. I couldn't stop thinking about what Shelly said to me earlier.

"Liam is mine, so stay away from him. He wouldn't fall in love with a sadist like you, who isn't even half as attractive as me," she has said.

I don't know why but her words are still bothering me. I don't love Liam, we are just friends. Why do I feel bad whenever I see Shelly getting closer to him?

"Still thinking about Liam?" Mike asked as he sat next to me.

"I wasn't thinking about Liam, and I don't like him that way, we're just friends." I tried to convince him and myself too.

He did not believe a word I said.

"Let me tell you something about him, and then you can decide whether or not you have feelings for him," Mike said.

"Liam is a nice guy at heart, it's just that he never lets anybody into his life because he's afraid they'll hurt him," Mike explained.

"What do you mean by hurting him?" I inquired.

"You know, his parents are always travelling and they never spend much time with him. He has never really got the love he deserves," he explained.

"But I've met his mother, and she seemed very loving to me," I said.

"It is just to show the outside world that they are one big happy family," Mike said.

"You know, he has never been in love in his life until a couple of months ago, and I have seen him change for the better," he added.

I don't love Liam

I don't love Liam

I don't Love Liam

I kept chanting to myself.

"Are you even listening?" Mike said, waving his hand in front of my face. "Who is that girl?" I asked, masking my emotions well.

"I'm sorry, I can't tell you that. He has asked me not to tell anyone," he answered.

"That's alright. I was just curious. Anyway, I'm really sleepy now. Good night, Mike!"

"Good night! Sleep well!"

Mike's POV

Alina almost ran back to her room after listening to everything I said about Liam. I believe I did the right thing by telling her. It is very evident that she cares for him more than a friend. I hope she realises this soon.

Alina's POV

I'm not sure why I feel sad knowing Liam is in love with someone. I should feel happy for him. Why am I feeling this way?

It was late and I couldn't sleep. I wanted to talk to somebody so I called Poppy.

"Hey, were you sleeping?" I asked her.

"No, I was washing my clothes at two in the morning. OF COURSE I WAS SLEEPING!"

"I'm sorry for waking you up, I'll call you in the morning," I said.

"No, Ally, I'm wide awake now thanks to you. Tell me why you called me at 2 a.m.," she replied.

"Um, I have a few issues and I'd like your advice," I explained nervously.

"Is it about Liam?" she questioned.

"Yes, how do you know that?" I replied.

"I am your best friend Ally, and I have seen how you look at him and vice versa."

"How do I look at him?" I asked, perplexed.

"With adoration and affection," she replied, smiling.

"No, I don't," I blushed.

"Yes, Ally, just admit it," she began teasing me.

"I think I should have been happy when Mike told me Liam is in love with someone, but all I felt was a fire in the pit of my stomach," I finally told her.

"That is because you love him. Stop denying it and tell him how you feel. Take a chance, Alina," she said."

"Do you know why you couldn't get intimate with Luke? It was because you never loved him. You were with him because you were afraid to tell him otherwise. You would have been with Liam if you hadn't hated him for what he did to Lucy. I know it was wrong, but I feel like he never did it on purpose, and Lucy has long forgiven him and moved on. Also Alina, I can see it in his eyes that he loves you. He will never hurt you." I tried holding back my tears when she said this.

"Thank you Poppy, I'll think about it," I said.

"I'll always be there for you Ally, good night!" she said.

"Good night," I said and hung up.

I believe Poppy is right. l am happy whenever I am with him. I should tell him how I feel.

26

I went downstairs to have breakfast. Mike was there too.

"Morning, Mikey!" I grabbed a cup of coffee for myself.

"Morning! Did you sleep well?"

"Yes, after that never ending lecture from you, I got a really good sleep, *grandpa!*" I love that annoyed face he makes every time I tease him.

"I shouldn't have said anything to you, but, thank you for hearing me out last night," he murmured.

"What did I miss? What happened last night?" Liam suddenly entered the kitchen.

"You know cutie here, um… she she was not sure about the difference between a banana cake and a banana pie. I was explaining that to her," Mike fumbled and I looked at him shocked.

Liam turned to me and asked, "is that it Al?"

"Um.. yeah. I've always been confused between the two," I said trying hard not to laugh.

"You guys need therapy. I can book an appointment if you say," he said.

"Good morning! Are you guys having fun without me?" Shelly entered and put her hand on Liam's shoulder. It really irritated me, it annoyed me to the extent that I couldn't control myself. I then did something very stupid. I walked towards Liam and kissed him on his cheek.

"We were talking about how guys react if you kissed them unexpectedly" I said looking at Shelly. I had no idea what I was doing. She got so annoyed that she left the kitchen without saying a word. I then turned towards Liam. He looked at me surprised. I realised how stupid I've been and took a few steps back. .

"I'm so sorry. I just can't stand her at times," I said and ran out of the kitchen. I felt so embarrassed that I decided to go out of the house.

Liam's POV

"We were talking about how guys would react if you kissed them, unexpectedly," Alina said, smiling at Shelly. Alina looked at me after Shelly had left. I just couldn't believe she had kissed me, it felt surreal. When she saw my face, she quickly removed her hands from me and backed away a few feet." Um..sorry about that, I just can't stand her at times." I could see her blushing. She then bolted out of the kitchen.

"I think she's feeling the same way as you man," Mike said.

"I don't think so, but that was unexpected from her," I said, confused.

"Didn't you see she was so crazy when Shelly put a hand on your shoulder?" Mike said.

"Shut up Mike, I know she did it to upset Shelly because they both hate each other," I reassured him and left the kitchen.

Alina's POV

I went back inside the house and upstairs to the conservatory after walking for what seemed like hours. When I went in, I saw Liam standing by the glass window looking at the snowfall. I quietly made my way in and grabbed a book from the table. I was just about to leave when he said "Al "and I froze. my place.

"What will you wear tomorrow at the new year's party?" he asked, coming closer to me.

"I'm not sure whether it'll be a dress or jeans and a top," I replied.

"Oh, okay! I forgot to tell you that we have a dress code and a theme for tomorrow," he said.

"Is it so? What is the theme?" I asked.

"Rachel has decided that the colour will be turquoise, and the girls will be wearing off-shoulder frocks," he said.

"Oh that's a great colour, but a frock in winter?" I asked trying hard not to think about what I did earlier.." She is the one who plans everything and believe me, it is never a good idea to defy her," he said smiling

"Okay, but I'll have to go shopping. Would you come along?" I asked.

"I would have loved to accompany you but I have some arrangements to make. You can go with Mike," he said.

I went shopping with Mike yesterday; it was good to have him along, and I must admit, he has a better sense of fashion than I do.

I heard a knock on my door as I was still in bed scrolling through my phone. "Come in," I said as I got out of bed."Hey, you're awake, did you have breakfast?" Rachel inquired as she entered my room.

"No, I only woke up a few minutes ago, I'll eat later," I answered.

"So, are you excited for the party tonight?" she asked.

"I am very excited. What about you?"

"I am too, the boys are taking care of the décor, I just supervise. Would you want to get ready together?" She asked

"Sure, that would be fun. What time?" I asked.

"Let's say around 6 because the party will begin at 9."

"That sounds fine," I confirmed.

After talking for a while she left to check how the boys were doing. I was having lunch alone in the kitchen at around one. Everyone else was busy with the decorations.

"Hi Alina, what are you doing here alone?" Shelly asked.

"I think it is none of your business," I replied.

"That is true, and Liam is none of yours," she said, giving an evil smile.

"You better stay away from him, Alina," she said in a threatening tone.

"And why should I?" I asked.

"I will give you something you really want," she replied.

"And what is that?" I inquired. "And what is that?" I inquired.

"Being the only daughter, I can ask my father to give you 60% of the company shares, only if you leave Liam."

I was perplexed.

"Why would I need your father's company?" I asked.

"Because 'Campbell. Co' was originally your Dad's," she replied.

I was shocked to discover that Shelly was Mr. Lawrence's daughter.

I thought for a while and asked, " Do you promise me that?"

I noticed a smirk on her face as she took out a document from her bag and handed it to me.

"This is the contract. You can read it and sign next to where I have," she said.

All the conditions were there mentioned in the contract.

If I sign this, I will get what is rightfully mine. But I will have to let Liam go. I love him deeply and I still haven't expressed my feelings for him.

Flashback

I heard a knock on my door.

"Come in," I said. It was Liam. He came in and closed the door behind him.

"Hey Li-li, what a surprise, do you want something?" I asked.

"Uh, Alina, can we talk?" he asked.

"Sure," I said, and both of us sat down on a couch.

"About the kiss yesterday?" he continued. I tensed up.

"I fell in love with you the first time I saw you, and I really really like you Alina, but I don't know if you feel the same way that is why I never confessed. Things were not the same before but we're friends now. I don't want to spoil our friendship but I like you more than a friend Al and I want to know how you feel," he said.

I went speechless for a while.

"Liam, what will happen to our relationship if my answer is not yes?" I asked, worried.

"We will always be friends Al, no bad feelings, just forget about what happened today," he assured me.

"Can I take some time to answer?" I asked.

"Take all the time you want," he replied.

Flashback ends

What makes me happier, money or the love of my life? I know if I sign this, my mother will no longer have to struggle and will be able to enjoy her life.

I picked up the pen and made my decision, my hand shivered as I signed that contract.

27

Hey Al! Come on in. I just finished cleaning my room," Liam said.

"Hi, Liam! Can we talk about earlier?" I asked hesitatingly.

"Sure." He looked happy.

He must be thinking that I'll tell him I like him too.

"Liam, can we be just friends since I...I...I don't like you the way you do." I felt my heart shattered as I said that. I wanted to tell him I love him, I wanted to scream this to the world but I couldn't, I couldn't because of that stupid contract. He looked devastated. I had never seen him look so sad.

"Oh! That… okay." He couldn't finish his sentence. I saw tears in his eyes.

"I thought you had the same feelings. Never mind," he said and a tear rolled down his cheek. "I was so stupid to think that way," he blabbered. "I'm sorry!" I said and ran away to my room. I couldn't control my tears anymore.

Liam's POV

I felt like someone repeatedly stabbed me using a knife. I know I shouldn't have kept my hopes high. I felt like my lungs were constricting so much that I couldn't breathe. I feel numb.

"Hey man, I am done bl..." Mike stopped in the middle of his sentence, came towards me and put a hand on my shoulder. "Hey what happened?" He asked.

"I feel I am incapable of love. Alina told me she doesn't like me"

"Hey, but i tho.."

"You keep your thoughts to yourself. I should have never listened to you and confessed my feelings."

Alina's POV

"Hey, wake up. We gotta get ready," said Rachel.

I slowly woke up. "Why don't you shower and get dressed? I will do your hair and makeup," .

I nodded and went to the bathroom. Rachel kept on talking, .I just sat there listening to her. It took us about an hour or two to get ready.

" You look stunning in that dress," she said. I gave her a half hearted smile and we headed to the conservatory where the party was being hosted.

When we entered the party, I saw Evan coming towards us.

"Hey, you look great!" he said.

"You look great too," I replied.

He gave Rachel a kiss and then took us to where the food was being served. I was not really hungry so I grabbed a flute of champagne and downed it. It made me feel lighter and so I took another one.

"Hey, Evan! How handsome you look!" I heard Shelly say.

I turned and saw Liam's hand wrapped around her waist and Shelly holding his arm. When Liam saw me looking, he kissed her on her cheeks and came towards me.

We greeted each other awkwardly. “So you and Shelly uh?” I asked playfully. It hurt me so much to say that.

“Yeah. After you left, she came and told me how much she loves me. I thought why not give it a chance.” “Yea, you are right,” I said smiling.

“Hey cutie, come on let's eat,” Mike said coming over to where we were standing. “Sure, come on Liam,” I said, and we went to have dinner.

It was one awkward dinner. Shelly was practically sitting on Liam's lap. I felt like strangling her. I felt angry at myself for agreeing to sign that contract. It was all my fault. It was my selfishness that had made me lose Liam..

After finishing the dessert all of us sat together to have drinks.

“I did not have the slightest idea of you two getting back together,” Evan said to Liam.

“Aren’t you happy for us, Evvy?” Shelly interrupted.

“It was Shelly’s idea. She thought we should give ourselves another chance, I felt she was right.” His voice sounded low.

“I thought you still love that girl. What happened to that?” asked Rachel.

“I don’t think we are destined to be together,” he replied. I tried hard to control my tears..

“Mike, what time are we going to leave at?” I asked, trying to change the conversation.

“I was thinking we should leave tomorrow evening. What do you guys think?” he asked.

Rachel and Evan had planned to visit her grandparents before leaving for London.

"So I think it would be just me, Alina and Liam. What about you, Shelly? Are you planning to stay here longer?" asked Mike.

"Actually, both Liam and I are planning to stay here for a couple of days. You and Alina can go ahead. We won't be coming," she said, smirking at me.

I felt myself burning. I wanted to shout out loud, I wanted to tell Liam that it was because of her that I had to distance myself from him and that I love him. I felt tied to some invisible chains that were weighing me down. My heart felt heavy. It was hard for me to hear anybody, I felt kind of zoned out.

"It's 11:55! Fireworks will begin. Let's go to the window," Rachel shouted, bringing me back to reality.

Mike and Evan started fighting over who will light the fireworks. Mike started jumping up and down like a kid, all of us burst into laughter.

"One minute left!" shouted Rachel. All of us were looking at the night sky waiting excitedly.

I heard Shelly saying something to Liam. When I turned around I saw she was standing just an inch apart from him. Her hand was inside his shirt and they were so close. Mike was holding her by the waist and with each passing second they were coming even closer.

Don't kiss her. Just don't!

I was screaming in my head.

Everybody started the countdown.

10...... 9.......

8...... Liam was looking at me.

7......

I am doing the right thing. I need to walk away

I tried very hard to not look at him.

6..... 5......

Shelly was now about to kiss him. I lost it then and stormed my way towards him, pushed her away and crashed my lips on his. He didn't kiss me back. He looked shocked.

SHIT! WHAT THE HELL DID I DO?

"I am so sorry. I was not.."

Before I could finish my sentence, he pulled me closer and kissed me, it felt as if this was what he was longing for. Right at that moment, fireworks started exploding.

"Happy New Year!" Everyone screamed. i

"I love you." I said looking deep into his eyes.

"What took you so long?" he said, smiling at me.

"You bitch! How dare you kiss my boyfriend? Did you forget the deal between us?" Shelly shouted at the top of her lungs.

I took the paper out of my bag and threw it in the fire.

"Shelly, I've realized that nothing is more important to me than Liam. I can earn money at any point in life but if I lose Liam now, I'll lose him forever. Even if you give me all the money in the world, I would still choose him. Him over anything else," I said.

"Tell her that you love me, and not her," she shouted at Liam.

"I never loved you Shelly. The only person I've ever truly loved is Alina. I'm sorry," Liam said.

She got enraged and ran out of the room.

I don't regret what I did. I can always earn money, I can find ways to keep my mother happy. What is the use of all the wealth when you can't have your loved ones by your side? Sacrificing my happiness for material things is the last thing I would do. With Liam by my side I felt I could be happy again. The pain of losing my father won't ever subside. I will always miss him. I did realize that I was ready to let my guard down and love again. Wherever my dad is, he must be happy seeing me with Liam. He must be watching over us from a place **far away,** with a contented smile. This thought made me feel I was right to choose Liam and with every step I take towards him I feel myself getting **yet closer.**

Memory

"Daddy I am scared. What if I fall?" I asked, sitting on my bicycle "Alina, don't worry! Daddy will be there for you no matter what. I will catch you if you fall." "You promise?" I asked. "I promise, cupcake!" he replied.

28

Hey Ally, morning! Want a ride to the beach party today?" asked Adrian.

"Sure," I said and started getting ready. . Liam was also coming. It has been five months since Liam, and I started seeing each other. It has not always been smooth for us but somehow we have managed to stick together through all the ups and downs.

"Alina! Darling, your friends are here!" my mom called. I quickly ran down the stairs, kissed her goodbye and left the house.

Lucy, Poppy and Adrian were there to pick me up. They looked much happier, much chirpier than usual.

"Why didn't Liam take you to the beach today? Did he refuse to?" Poppy asked teasingly.

"No, he didn't refuse to. He just told me that he had some arrangements to make, must be busy with something," I replied.

"Those arrangements better be good," said Adrian with a laugh.

I didn't quite get what she was saying and before I could ask, my phone rang. It was Mike.

"Hey, Mikey! What's up?"

"Hey, Cutie! I need you to call me up when you guys arrive at the beach? Can you do that for me, please?"

Something about his voice made me suspicious.

"Why? Why should I do that?"

"You ask so many questions. I wonder how Liam survives with you," he tried drifting off the topic.

"I won't do anything unless you tell me why." I said without giving up.

"Okay, but promise me you'll keep it just to yourself"

"I promise. C'mon, tell me now!" I tried keeping my voice low.

"I have planned a surprise for Lucy. We have been together for a month now, you know, I just wanted to make her feel special. Tell me as soon as you reach there," he said.

"Okay, I'll let you know," I tried keeping the conversation short so that nobody would suspect.

When we reached, I saw Mike standing in the parking lot. Lucy rushed towards him and hugged him.

They look so happy together. Ever since they have started dating, Mike gives all his time to Lucy. Liam doesn't even pick up my calls at times.

"Hey, Mikey!" I said

"Here, wear this before I forget," he handed me a blindfold. Not just Lucy but all of us were supposed to put those on. "Hurry up and put that on! I am not as patient as Beanie!"

Mike then guided us to the place where he had planned the surprise.

"You can remove it now," I heard a familiar whisper from behind.

I knew who it was, my heart jumped with joy.

Liam opened my blindfold and in front of me I saw a beautiful wooden tent house decorated with pink, red and white roses. There were hundreds of helium balloons floating all over the place. It all felt like a beautiful dream. It looked as if a fairytale had come alive. There was a cake kept inside the tent with my name on it. I knew this was the kind of moment that would make me smile for the rest of my life. I wanted to absorb every bit of it. I looked towards Liam and tears started rolling down my cheeks.

"You like it?" he asked.

I fell short of words, I did not know what to say. I just hugged him tight.

"I love you, Liam. Thank you!," I whispered in his ears.

"Alina, I'll always love you. I'll never let a tear fall from those beautiful eyes," Liam said with a kiss.

You make me so happy, the happiest I've ever been.

"Are you going to cut that cake or should I do that for you?" Mike asked and we all cracked up laughing.

"How do you guys remember my birthday? I never told you," I asked, surprised.

"Good friends have their own way of finding these things," Poppy said and gave me the warmest of hugs. Everybody else joined. I felt loved, I felt belonged and I was happy.

This was not the end of surprises, I had no idea all of them had brought gifts for me. Adrian gifted me a cute little bunny that she knew I had always wanted, and a basket full of my favourite chocolates. Mike and Lucy gave me a beautiful set of earrings, they were so beautiful I couldn't take my eyes off them. Poppy gave me a gift card from Kate Spade that she knew I was crazy about. Evan and Rachel gave me two tickets for a cruise, to spend my summer with Liam. I did not know how to tell them how special all of it made me feel.

Liam walked towards me with a black velvet box. Inside it there was an impossibly beautiful ring.

"This is not an engagement ring Alina, it's a promise ring. I promise to stick with you through all the thicks and thins, to support you and to be there for you whenever you need me," he said and placed the ring on my finger.

Before I could say anything, he came forward, held my hand and we kissed. It was a kind of kiss that will be etched in my memories forever. All of us then came together for a photograph. It was a kind of picture that I can smile looking at in the worst of my days. I'll always love the people who are in it and I'm sure they'll always love me too. Maybe what they say is actually true, everything does get better in the end.

MEET THE AUTHOR

Amina is an eighteen-year-old aspiring writer. She has been writing for almost a year now and has three novels completed and published on various online reading platforms.

Her journey doesn't end there, she wants to let the world read about what she writes and put a smile on people's faces. Her stories have a unique plot that would keep you coming back for more!

ACKNOWLEDGEMENTS

First and foremost I would like to thank my mother who was the only individual who encouraged me to write a novel which at first I never had any faith in myself, but she had been my pillar of support and encouragement. Next would be my English teacher Sherine Jemison. I think without her guidance I wouldn't have known how to write a book. Also, I would like to thank my best friend Mahnoor Ahmed I think without her in my life I wouldn't have experienced a lot of things, a friend who is straightforward and tells you when something is wrong, and my gorgeous aunt Shamirah Akbar Ali well I think everyone should have a person like her in your life.

That would be all the people who were there when I was writing the book, but I think the biggest credit goes to the Inkfeathers team who were the people who brought my book to life, and all the members of Inkfeathers who guided me through the entire publishing process.

INKFEATHERS PUBLISHING

India's Most Author Friendly Publishing House

Stay updated about latest books, anthologies, events, exclusive offers, contests, product giveaways and other things that we do to support authors.

Inkfeathers Publishing

@InkfeathersPublishing

@_Inkfeathers

@Inkfeathers

Inkfeathers.com

We'd love to connect with you!